THESE DARK
WINGS

Born and raised in Eastern Canada,
John Owen Theobald moved to the
UK to study the poetry of Keats, and
in 2009 received a PhD from the
University of St Andrews. He lives
in London, England.

'I really enjoyed this story. It reminded me somewhat of *The Book Thief*, with the subject matter and style of writing... The story is genuinely very sweet throughout, and I was impressed with how strongly it finished. The final twist is definitely worth it!'

K.S. Marsden

'Theobald's character development, text and his use of language is astounding.'

www.picksandreadsforkids.com

'The writing is deeply comfortable and easy to connect with. The story starts simply, but builds into something much more than I expected. It's atmospheric, absorbing, and brilliant! This is the sort of book my teacher used to read to my class in the last year of primary school – and she was very picky about her choice of book!'

Dawn

'I recommend this book 5/5. *These Dark Wings* is the most intriguing book I have ever read, I really connected to the characters and felt empathy for them. I really loved the flow of the story and what happened. My favourite part has to be the unexpected twist at the end... The character who I liked the most was Anna Cooper. The story is from Anna's view point, her job is to guard the ravens from death as legend has it that if all the ravens leave the tower Britain will fall. She faces many challenges including the people in the tower. Overall I want to say read the book, it is phenomenal!'

Dylan Christie, age 10

'This was a time where the population of the United Kingdom felt that they could be invaded at any moment. The author captures this tension really well, particularly as the first-person viewpoint adds a sense of immediacy to the story. The writing style and thoughtful construction with plenty of good dialogue and frequent breaks within chapters make this a highly approachable story to children, even those as young as nine.'

www.writecreating.wordpress.com

'I thought that this book was incredibly well written, it captured my attention and refused to let it go… If you read *The Book Thief* and enjoyed it then you will love this novel! The story is very sweet, touching and doesn't let go of your attention. It is a very strong and powerful book which has an incredible ending.'

Sophie Narey

'This book is fantastic! I truly could not put it down. I've been looking for the next great youth series and this is it. I need to read the next instalment and am keeping my fingers crossed that it comes out soon. Anna is a smart and curious protagonist and following her explorations of the mysteries of the tower is an absolute delight!'

Katherine Barcsay

'A great read! As a schoolteacher, I am always searching for good books to use as teaching tools. This book would be excellent to use for discussions on how the Blitz affected children. I know the children would love Anna's character. Can't wait for book 2!'

Wendy McIntyre

JOHN OWEN THEOBALD

THESE DARK
WINGS

HEAD
of ZEUS

9 7 5 3 4 6 8

A catalogue record for this book is available from
the British Library.

Map and feather © Sarah Carter

Paperback ISBN 9781784974367
Ebook ISBN 9781784974299
Hardback ISBN 9781784974312

Printed and bound by CPI Group (UK) Ltd, Croydon, CR0 4YY

Supported using public funding by
**ARTS COUNCIL
ENGLAND**

Head of Zeus Ltd
First Floor East
5–8 Hardwick Street
London EC1R 4RG
WWW.HEADOFZEUS.COM

For Nana

If the ravens leave the Tower, the kingdom will fall...

TOWER
OF LONDON

1. WHITE TOWER

2. CHAPEL

3. BARRACKS

4. HOSPITAL

5. ROOST

6. TOWER GREEN

7. KING'S HOUSE

8. CONSTABLE TOWER

9. SALT TOWER

10. BLOODY TOWER

11. MAIN GUARD

12. CASEMATES

13. TOWER SCHOOL

14. TRAITORS' GATE

15. DEVELIN TOWER

16. BRASS MOUNT

17. WEST GATE

18. MOAT

19. RIVER THAMES

17

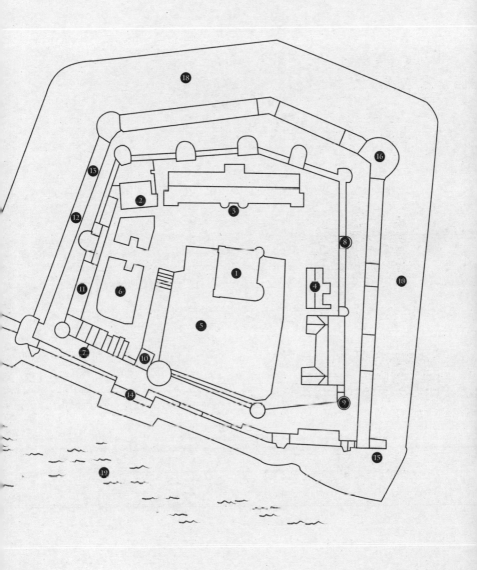

In England they're filled with curiosity.
They keep asking, 'Why doesn't he come?'
Be calm, be calm. He's coming.

Hitler, Berlin rally, 4 September 1940

There were three ravens sat on a tree.
They were as black as black could be.
Then one of them said to his mate,
Where shall we our breakfast takc?

The Three Ravens, English folk ballad

I

THE TOWER AND
THE PRISON

These cruel, wanton, indiscriminate bombings of London are, of course, a part of Hitler's invasion plans. He hopes, by killing large numbers of civilians, and women and children, that he will terrorize and cow the people of this mighty imperial city. Little does he know the spirit of the British nation, and the tough fibre of Londoners.

Churchill, radio broadcast, 11 September 1940

1

Friday, 4 October 1940

The shelter was under the playing fields at school. We weren't inside for long, but it was sunny and I felt every minute in the hot darkness. Hitler had started bombing in the daytime. Afterwards I heard that a shell had hit near our street, and some motor cars and a bus had crashed. People were killed. My form teacher told me that. Bus 414, she said.

All I thought of at the time was how much better the school shelter was than the flimsy Anderson shelter in the garden (*always* filled with spiders and earwigs), and that Mum would be happy I was here. I did not think of where Mum was.

It wasn't so close, but she liked the walk to the Underground. Mum only caught the bus to the tube station if the hot water had run out or breakfast had been burnt. She worked at the *Evening Standard*, as a journalist. I said it was all a mistake, that Mum was fine. Maybe she had not gone into work at all today. If they'd just let me go home, she would be in the kitchen making cheese on toast, worried about *me*.

I wasn't allowed to go home.

Long after all the other kids had left, I stayed at school, wishing that my best friend Flo could be with me, but she was already on her ship to Montreal. I sat in the office with the headmaster, who watched me from over his papers with a queer expression. Even though I still had my book on the Stuarts from Mr Fenwick's history class, all I could do was stare at the words – strange, meaningless.

Then someone from the Women's Voluntary Service came and sat in the chair next to mine. I was told that, during the incident, Mum had been on bus 414. I was told that on Friday, 27 September, Mum had died.

It wasn't possible. It simply... wasn't. The headmaster smiled weakly, the woman not at all, and the sun was bright at the window and I was still at school.

Raids at least happen quickly. They are endless, of course, but things change – die, explode, vanish. In that chaos, things *happen*. That afternoon, nothing happened at all. I stayed in the office.

When night finally came, back down to the shelter we all went. That raid was one of the worst. I sat on the hard bench with the headmaster and the serious woman, the warden leaning against the wall. An old man, I remember, tried to push inside carrying a cage with a budgie in it.

The warden shook his head. He didn't even move from the wall.

'You can't bring that in now, can you, sir?'

That made me sad. I wanted to say something, to yell out, to beg them to let the man and his stupid bird come inside. They didn't come back but a few others arrived, and soon it was warm and clammy with all the bodies. The warden, in his overalls, wellies, and steel helmet, must have been sweating. I sat in silence as the raid pounded on.

In the morning, I was in the office again. Someone else from the WVS came, with the same purple and bottle-green uniform. She held out a bag of things from the house. My blue hairbrush, Pond's cold cream, some pictures (not the coloured photograph of Mum sitting at the kitchen table with Father and me – where Mum looks like Vivien Leigh but with fox-coloured hair).

Clutching the bag, I was ushered into the darkness of a taxi.

Crrruck. Crrruck.

The croaking of the ravens drags me into the present. No more memories: this is my life now. My old life ended a long month ago on that horrible day.

I stomp my feet in the cold dawn air, and inch closer

to the series of giant, open-air cages built into the ancient wall of the Tower of London.

Crrruck. Crrruck.

Yes, yes, I am coming. I walk forward, shoulders tightened, and wrench open the stiff wire gate. If ravens are so smart, how come they do nothing all day but bury the same scrap of food over and over again? If they're really such 'sophisticated birds', why can't they understand the simplest gesture? No, Uncle Henry must have got a piece of shrapnel in the head. The Tower ravens are just as dumb as any other bird.

Greedier, though. And feeding them is my job.

'Good morning, MacDonald.'

The great head turns, studies both me and the chopped meat, deciding which is the meal. Then the razor beak begins tearing and pulling, eyes never leaving mine. *For now*, the look says. I fill the water bowl and move on. Black eyes follow me.

The sun begins to rise. High above, the day looks like it will be empty, clear. Down here, mist still clings to the stone. The White Tower, the oldest, tallest building – the heart of the Tower of London – is also the home of the ravens. As I reach the second raven, a shiver runs through me. I am cold, not *afraid*. They are only birds.

I yank open the cage. Croaks issue from the dark before the large bird strides free. He pauses, gazing over the Green, before turning to his meal. I try to keep my voice neutral.

'Good morning, Edgar.'

I receive only a sideways glance for my role as servant.

'Just feed the ravens,' Uncle answers whenever I start to ask questions. 'Remember their names, and give them their meal.'

Uncle Henry is an important man in the Tower. Everyone calls him 'Ravenmaster'. He says I am brave for a little girl – I am *not* little, I am almost thirteen – and so he can trust me with the dawn feeding. But I know there are other reasons. When I was first brought here, Uncle proudly marched with the sunrise. Each day he came to the roost later and later, his hat sliding down his tired face. Now he does not come at all.

I can handle feeding some giant birds. The bucket is heavy, the measurements confusing, but I have learned these past weeks. Hold the bucket grip in the middle, let it swing with your steps – that way, the mess will not slop over the rim. *Never* forget your gloves. The leather is warm, the cage wires cold, and the ravens' beaks like metal. Always they are sharpening their beaks.

At least four ounces of raw meat (Uncle chopped it last night) and two biscuits, soaked in blood, placed well out of reach. Much easier than the evening feed, which Uncle still does, when the birds are alert and irritable. They hate the bombs as much as the rest of us.

Greet each bird by name.

'Hello, Cora.'

A girl bird, as if it makes any difference. Even though I

have tried to imagine her croak as softer, lighter than the others, it is the same low, gurgling noise from deep in the throat. *Orrk. Orrk.* Grey breath steams from her black beak.

'Be honest with me, Cora. Uncle is only teasing, isn't he? I mean, can *you* really be a Guardian of the Empire? You're a bird, and a bird that can't even fly.'

A cold wind blows against the castle.

'You're up early.'

Startled, I turn to face the voice.

'Yeoman Oakes,' I say, controlling my fear. 'Good morning.'

'We should always carry our masks, Anna.'

Oakes holds up a black mask attached to a strap at his shoulder, and offers a smile as unconvincing as my own.

I stare, hunting for the proper words. In his Warder uniform – dark blue coat with a red crown on it, long cloak and stiff hat – Oakes is strict and imposing, like a painting of an old king.

'I know, Yeoman Oakes, sir. I forgot this morning. I am sorry.'

'Well,' he says, watching the birds at their breakfast with a frown, 'they are the real Beefeaters of the Tower, are they not? I must go and see if there's any toast for us humans.'

Oakes heads off to the kitchen.

Ruffled, I lift the heavy bucket, continuing down the line.

I am forced to carry the black mask everywhere, the bloody nuisance, in case Hitler puts poison gas in the bombs. Everywhere I go, the mask must come in the cardboard box. Oakes is such a misery about it. Mum always carried hers. I can see her, in her Burberry and rubbers, mask over her shoulder. It didn't help.

And I am *not* up early. Every morning I must be at the roost for dawn. Yeoman Oakes knows that. He practically follows Uncle Henry around. Likely, habit brought him here looking for Uncle. Was that why he gave me such a queer look? Did he forget that I help with the morning feeding? That I can do it just fine on my own?

He's right about breakfast, though. Toast and an egg, tea without a spoon of sugar, and yet there is food for these birds. How is that fair? How can we care about birds when *people* are dying?

Uncle has told me why, though I don't believe him.

Always there have been six ravens at the Tower. If the Tower ravens fly away, the kingdom will fall. What does that mean? How can a bunch of croaking birds protect us from bombs and poison gas? My mind swings around slowly. Without them, we would have no King or Queen, no London or Edinburgh? What would there be instead? Germany? Nothing? I'm not sure I want to know the answer.

Taking a long breath of the morning air, I release the next bird, Merlin, avoiding the black swamp of his eyes. On each of them the flight wing is clipped, so they can't get any proper height. Mainly they swoop and perch on the low branches and battlements, sometimes reaching a turret or rooftop. The ravens *could* fly away, Uncle says, but it is not a serious worry. Well fed and looked after, they have no desire to become just a common bird.

The cages are for their own safety. Foxes sneak inside somehow – I remember Uncle saying, in his official tour-guide voice, 'The Tower is a place of great secrets and mysteries, of countless hidden passageways and tunnels.' Uncle insists that, far from being prisoners, the ravens are in fact happy. Special.

Oakes gave a different reason. One night after dinner, his face splotchy and red, he leaned across the table: 'The birds will not leave. They came here for the corpses. Their big dinner is coming.' He laughed as if this were funny.

Happily, I approach the final cage, the now light bucket swaying with each step. This visit is the only reason I am able to make it through this dreary task. I always save it for last.

'Good morning, Grip and Mabel.'

I cannot tell them apart by *look*, but they behave as complete opposites. The two birds are mated – they are both ten – and while Grip is angry and mean, Mabel is quiet and calm. She always responds to Uncle's 'secret whistle,' leaving whatever she is burying to collect her meal. She does not look at me like the other birds do.

I pry open the tight hinge, which screams as it swings. Grip is out in a flash, blinking in the light. Ravens blink sideways, like some sort of feathered lizard.

Crrruck. Crrruck.

'Good morning, Mr Grip. And where is your lovely wife? Waiting to take her meal inside the cage? Not ripping everything apart in front of me? Well, I know why *she's* my favourite. Manners make the bird, you know.'

Showing Mabel the same courtesy, I peer inside the cage, alerting her to my presence before I enter. I can't do Uncle's secret whistle anymore than I can fly. Mabel is not grubby or horrid. She is proof that life in the Tower is possible. It is because of her that I have not gone mad in this place.

The bucket slips from my hand, clatters on its side. For a long moment I can only stare. All around ravens croak madly, knowingly.

Crrruck. Crrruck.

The cage is empty.

Mabel is gone.

Don't worry about Mabel. She'll be back.

I'm the one who's leaving.

Uncle will not be coming to breakfast. Not because he's

upset about the lost bird – he knew all about that, though it surprised me when he said so. But, of course, he had put the ravens to bed and Mabel had not been among them. He'd hoped that she might be found sunning herself on the ramparts this morning. He did not seem worried when she wasn't. Lying still, eyes almost closed, he smiled.

'She'll turn up. Just worry about the others for now.'

But I hear something else, something he didn't say. If the Tower ravens leave, the kingdom will fall. Well, there are still five ravens here, croaking and flapping. Surely five are enough. *Just eat your toast.*

Like all the other rooms here, the kitchen in the Bloody Tower is made of smooth stone. Patches of white but mostly dark stone, climbing up to a huge vaulted ceiling. The stained-glass window pours down sparkling red and blue light. I had no idea how freezing it could be indoors. A thousand years old. All of that cold trapped inside the stone itself.

A large fireplace with too few logs extends into the room. All I want is to crouch down beside it. Instead I take my place on the bench, as far from Oakes as I can be. An empty, musty smell battles with the cooking eggs. At least I can put the gas mask on the floor.

Without Uncle's smiling presence the kitchen is gloomy. Smoke clouds the damp air. Little can be seen aside from the small glow of pipes and cigarettes, washed in colour from the stained glass. Stony voices echo through the room.

'Didn't I tell you? The railings are gone, and suddenly everyone is walking across the grass.'

'It's a short cut.'

'The green plots are not to be walked over.'

The Warders are a prickly lot, and it is strange to see them out of uniform. In regular suits and ties, they look almost... normal. There's no talk of the missing bird. Uncle alone seems to care about them.

Oakes stares at the wall as he chews. The stiff hat is gone, but he is the only one in his uniform. Oakes is tall and freckled, his hair thin and brown. He might be Uncle's age, though he looks older. Where Uncle is round and sturdy, Oakes is all straight lines and angles. Even his eyes are dark and strict. Always he wears an expression as if he is looking at something but not quite sure what it is. *It is a wall.*

Warders with families eat in their own kitchens. The bachelors come here; I don't know why. In addition to Uncle and Oakes, there is Mr Cecil – Mr Cecil's wife died of illness years ago and his sons are old enough to be in the war, so he is all alone; and giant Mr Brodie with his almost crooked nose, whose wife and son actually live in the Tower, but who is here at every breakfast anyway.

Knives scrape plates. My thoughts are drawn again to Mabel – how she and Grip would hook beaks and play. Is she gone? Has she really escaped?

'A fine room,' Mr Brodie says in a ringing voice. It is clear that he is talking to me. 'Medieval, you know. Well, except for the ceiling. Some modern adjustments are necessary at times.' He leans in, as if imparting a great secret. 'Had two Archbishops of Canterbury in this room. Not bad, as far as prisons go.'

I take the fork from out of my mouth. 'It is a beautiful room, Yeoman Brodie.'

Even if the company was more welcoming, with food being so scarce one prefers to eat in private. Flo would have been great at this. Even before the Blitz, she ate slower than anyone I've ever seen. Once she carried the same banana from her bedroom to the parlour, taking a bite and putting it down again, as it turned all spotted and black. Cherries she ate like they were little apples.

Now the Warders are arguing. I hear occasional shouts of laughter, but Yeoman Oakes has an angry tone. Each time he brings his head forward to speak, I see the empty spot of hair. I focus on the mugs, the table.

'That is what a leader is for,' Oakes is saying.

'For making peace with Hitler?'

'For putting an end to the U-boat blockade, Brodie, so the people can eat. Putting an end to this bombing, so people stop dying in the streets. What will protect us from a two-thousand-pounder? These walls?'

Suddenly Oakes turns and faces me. I sit up with a jolt. That long, triangular face staring into mine. I look back through the smoke in surprise.

'Sir?' I say.

'People – a certain kind of people – find Churchill

inspirational. Well, here's your chance to see for your-self.'

I quickly look down again, wishing he would go back to his wall. What is he talking about? *He is mad.*

'Thousands of innocent people, mothers and fathers, brothers and sisters – they have homes, families, all the things that make life worth living.' His voice is very loud now, loud and grating. 'They didn't want this war. They didn't want the slaughter of their neighbours, of their communities. And our planes are the same to the German people. Right now, perhaps, a girl in Berlin looks up from her window in terror, waiting for our bombs to fall.'

'Gregory, that's quite enough,' Brodie interrupts.

Oakes half stands, pointing a long finger at him.

'That's no more than Margaret Cooper would have said, and quite right. Imagine what she would write about this mess.'

I am stunned by the sound of Mum's name. No one, not even Uncle, has spoken her name aloud. Why is Oakes talking about her? Then, before fully rising to leave, he mutters darkly.

'Are we ready for an invasion?'

In the silence, I feel the chill of the stone underfoot.

Mr Brodie clears his throat. 'Nevertheless, it will be an

honour to host the prime minister. He is due to visit us Sunday next, as Yeoman Oakes mentioned. I think you will enjoy it very much, Anna. And your uncle should be feeling a sight better by then.'

I try to smile back. I don't care about seeing the prime minister. Why would he come here anyway? *And how dare Oakes talk about Mum?*

Mr Brodie is still watching me. 'And you must be looking forward to Monday. Starting school again?' He smiles kindly. 'Be around some children your own age, and away from grouchy old men.'

'Yes, thank you, sir. I'm looking forward to the new school.'

I know nothing of the school – not even where to find it in the castle. And why do classes start so late? It would be nearly half term at home.

He is still looking at me, waiting. *What do people even talk about in this place?*

'Bloody Tower is very old, isn't it, Yeoman Brodie? Were the ravens here even before that?'

His eyes go wide. 'The ravens?'

'Uncle says the ravens have been here a long time. That the legend of the ravens goes all the way back to Charles II. Maybe even further.'

'Legend of the… Well, your uncle would be the one to know about all that.'

He sounds slightly uncomfortable, but now that we are talking about it, I *do* have a question to ask.

18

'So if the ravens are gone, London – and Manchester and Glasgow, and all of Britain – will surrender?'

He frowns, grows more serious. 'Britain is more than London and Glasgow. It is a Commonwealth that spans the world. It is an idea, a shared culture.'

The Warders rise and begin cleaning. Without wives, they do their own washing up, before changing into their uniforms for Chapel and then heading off to their posts.

A sudden noise. We all turn.

Every sound seizes the mind, focuses it. Within the great ceilings and halls of the Tower, sounds bounce off beams and leak through stone. In the seconds before a name can be put to each noise – a dropped pot, a slammed door, a calling raven – other, sinister words float to the surface. *Engine, bomb, shrapnel.*

I reach for the mask, suddenly thankful that Oakes monstered on about it. Even Mr Brodie, despite all his brave talk and giant size, freezes with pipe to his lips, dripping dish over the sink, turning his eyes to mine. I know it as well as he does. Bombs do not care if you are a soldier or a cook, a mother or a child. A Warder or a girl.

No one is more protected than another. And no one can protect another.

But the ravens, Uncle claims, *can*. They can sense the shift in the air, notice changes in the sky that aircraft spotters are blind to, and other such rubbish talk. One thing is true: when ravens are upset, you know it. The strange, deep, horrible croak becomes something else

– high-pitched and wild. A shriek, almost human.

The sound outside *is* a raven, croaking just beyond the Green. What does it mean? It is, I somehow know for certain, a message for us.

A warning? Or a threat?

The ravens are here for the corpses. Their big dinner is coming.

The Warders are everywhere. Even during Chapel, they are posted at all the exits. From one end of the Tower to the other, inside the walls and out, men in blue coats stand guard. And you never know where another will suddenly appear – around a corridor, from the top of a stone staircase. They are always there, waiting, searching.

I will never get past them.

I have sneaked into the library and read as much history as I could stand in order to find proof – proof that it can be done. One prisoner convinced a group of friends to lower him down into a waiting boat. Another – some lord, I think – was brought a disguise of women's clothes by his wife and servants, who then smuggled him out.

Both had help. Family. Friends. A boat. I have no one, nothing.

Mabel, how did you do it? A flightless bird got out and I cannot.

Is it a sign? Is Mabel giving me hope, that I too can escape the coming bombs and fire? Maybe Uncle *was* right and Mabel knew more – she *sensed* something coming, something about to happen. She escaped to save herself. To show me the way.

It is impossible.

I stand staring, defeated. A vast, curving, snaking pile of rock: towers, arches, ramparts and passageways too narrow for cats. Stone stretching out, east and west, north and south, huge, windowless walls climbing upward, hiding the city, the sun, the world. Along with the gas mask, I must always carry a whistle, in case I get buried in the debris of a bomb. Now I feel that it is too late. *I am already buried.*

And, of course, it rains every day so I can go nowhere without my umbrella. Turning away from the stone walls, I walk towards the Green. My days, after prowling the castle in vain for freedom, are spent here, wet and alone. Alone, that is, except for the wandering, muttering ravens with their *orrk, orrk*, as they potter about, or the harsh *kraa*.

The rain falls harder. The towers look even more dreary in this weather. As I gaze around, a stunned feeling rises up, making it difficult to do anything at all. Thoughts become as heavy and grey as the stones.

How dare Oakes talk about Mum.

What was he even talking about? 'Making peace with Hitler,' Yeoman Brodie said, but Oakes mumbled about an invasion. *He is mad.*

The rain grows until it bounces off my umbrella like a drum. Only for the briefest moment does it sound like approaching bombers. I shut my eyes against the rain, trying to imagine that I am not surrounded by croaking shadows and endless walls. Then comes a real sound, a human sound.

Clicking footsteps.

It is Nell. She is older, roughly the same age as the NAAFI girls who work in the canteen. Far too old to speak to me. Where exactly she lives and what exactly she does is a mystery. Mainly, she stands around and smokes cigarettes, looking very trim. Now she is wearing a lovely blue and white hairband as she saunters across the passage. No sign of a gas mask.

A black flash tugs away my gaze. Where the ravens come from, I can't tell. They can't fly, but they can *swoop*, a dark blur in the corner of your eye. Somehow, despite their size, they arrive unseen, appearing as if they were always there. Only the ravens' voices – their dreadful, gnarled voices – tell you where they are.

'Where are *you* from?'

I turn, quickly. For a horrifying minute I worry that I was thinking aloud – or, worse, acting like Uncle and talking to the ravens – but Nell looks unconcerned. She doesn't even have the small, bloodshot eyes of the rest of us. She wears a thin necklace that looks almost like pearls.

'Maida Vale,' I say, my voice higher than usual. 'Warwick Avenue.'

'Knew it.'

She takes a long haul off her cigarette.

'It's too bad you had to come here. Where the bombs fall.'

'Are you from here?' I ask, as if her jumbled Cockney accent is possible to ignore. I feel thoroughly second hand.

I nod when she does, unsure what to say next. Should I stand? Offer her my umbrella? My face is red and stiff from the wind. *I need sleep*. I say nothing.

'So, what are you doing here?' A pencilled eyebrow is raised. 'You look after the birds now?'

I try to answer but am forced to wait as the great clock on top of the barracks strikes 11 a.m. She ashes her cigarette briskly.

'Yes,' I say into the still ringing air. 'My uncle – Henry Reed, the Yeoman Warder, if you know him – he is the Ravenmaster. Which I suppose makes me the junior Ravenmaster.'

'It's not all that fun,' I add, for some reason. 'A lot of the time it's just cleaning the cages.'

She laughs, really slow. 'Yeah, some folk can't even clean up after themselves.'

I laugh too. 'I don't much like them, to be honest. Well,

'I like Mabel, but…' Is my voice always so weak, so small? 'The job's not all bad. They are quite smart, actually, if not as smart as Uncle says. You'd think they were smarter than people, the way he goes on about them. I'm called Anna, by the way. Anna Cooper.'

But Nell is done with her cigarette and our talk, and after a final narrowed glance at the ravens, she turns and clicks back across the passage. Again I am alone. I sit, hunched under the grey clouds and the deliberately cold rain, watching the smoke climb from her discarded cigarette.

Suddenly I cannot breathe.

All this stone – stone covering everything – makes me feel *shadowed*, and dark and old and caged. The bricks blackened and crusted, gnawed by the wind and rain for a thousand years. It will take time to 'grow accustomed' to the Tower, Uncle says. *I never will.*

Why did Mum leave me here, in this horrible place? In this world without her?

2

The night is silent. Only the distant waves pushing though the dark. From the east come the sounds of the river, lapping waves and foghorns, dockers' voices and crying gulls. The waves. The water. The sea. *Father.*

Don't let your imagination get away from you, Mum used to say.

I am just exhausted. Too exhausted to sleep.

I sit up on the bunk, which creaks in protest. The hardest bed in the world, with barely enough space to put my knees up (I can only sleep with my knees up). I have not unpacked my pyjamas, but wear my clothes in any event, my ID card and whistle in the pocket of my jumper. It is freezing and at any moment I will have to stumble down to the shelter.

I fumble for the candle, light it. The room around me is dark and empty. Dust covers everything. My hair, no longer red, is now a dull grey like everything else. I don't bother having the electric light on, terrified that in the rush to the shelter I'll forget to switch it off. Even with the curtains drawn properly, it is not worth the risk.

My throat is clogged from the dust and my stomach heaves horribly – a much larger butter ration is needed to make the wartime bread edible. I think of the food at Flo's house. They had me for dinner a lot – Mum never came, I think maybe she was sad not to have Father with her – and Mrs Swift would always send me home with lots of leftover roast beef. Once she gave me a whole jar of pickles and, beaming, I carried it up the driveway. I remember being quite cross with Mum when she just shoved it in the cupboard without a word.

This is my home now. I know billeting officers come to houses and tell people they have to take someone in (like the giant Canadian soldier that Katherine Molesworth's family had to put up in their study), but surely London has other spare rooms than this frozen chamber in the Bloody Tower. The window faces west, away from most of the bombing. If I look I can just see Tower Hill beyond. I don't look.

A mouse is in my room, scurrying against the wall, a dark smudge in the shadows. Why don't the ravens eat it? If I could catch it, I would happily present Grip with this gift. Mice lived in the Underground shelter too, squeaking and scratching, their horrible long tails vanishing into impossible cracks.

I think for a moment of the stories of the young princes – two boys my own age – who disappeared in this very tower. Not disappeared, I know. *Those boys were murdered*, comes Oakes's voice. *That's why they call it the Bloody Tower.*

I can't stay here, sleeping in a chamber in the bloody Bloody Tower. I can't adjust to this. If home is destroyed, I will go to Montreal. Flo is there. No dirty great bombs or ghastly cold towers or creaking wooden bunks. I will write to her now, tell her that I am coming.

I hold the dusty diary in my hand. It was in my bag, that day in the shelter, so I have kept it with me. Instead of writing anything new, I turn blackened pages, flipping through the past year.

One entry, just before Mum's accident, is a list. We had done it in school (Irene started it, I think), and filled in the blanks at home:

> *I like the feeling of speeding on the Bakerloo Line.*
> *I wish that I had less (fewer?) freckles.*
> *Examinations (and sharks) make me nervous.*
> *I would love to learn to drive a train.*

'Drive a train?' I don't care if I never go down into the Underground again. 'Sharks'? I only want one more day in bed at home, with Mum's slow voice reading to me.

I exhale deeply, trying to keep calm.

But I am trapped here. Another day and another day and another day. Changeless, from the morning feeding to the night raids to the potato dinners. I am stuck in this room with the windows covered, smothering me. And even if I could fall asleep, the dreams would be there, waiting.

No. I am not a child. I am here, behind solid walls, with at least a little warmth. Countless people want to go home but cannot. *Some people have nothing but what they stand up in.*

I shut the diary, pressing it closed. I must keep my thoughts focused – or a cold sea of panic starts to rise.

The Tower is not so rotten. Even if Nell and the Warders are mean sometimes, I can still hear the distant rumble of traffic outside the walls if I listen hard. With the dark, the world drops away. But it is still there.

Flo said I was special, that it was unlucky to have brothers and sisters like she did, that I would never be left out of things. What things? If I had a sister (I'd never want a brother) she would be here now. A friend. A friend to keep away this mouse.

I saw Flo before she left. She had her father's suitcase, covered in stickers from faraway hotels. She didn't seem too sad. Neither did I, of course. We just planned where we would meet.

'Outside the Notre-Dame Basilica,' she said. 'On the steps.'

I agreed, not knowing what the basilica was but sure that I could find it.

'Will you learn French?' I asked. I had only ever met one French person before, Mr Pepin, who made a chair for Mum. I couldn't understand a word he said.

She paused to think. 'Maybe by then, yeah. Don't worry, I'll teach you.'

I can see them now, Flo with her sister and two brothers – both older, short and wide, and not like her at all – all of them playing together in the quiet streets of Montreal.

There will never be a house like ours there. With a small garden with sweet peas and the skinny magnolia tree, never quite as pink as Mrs Weber's across the street. Old Mrs Morgan and her terrier next door. The photograph of us, of the family together.

All that is gone.

For now I am safe. And I must try to sleep. I blow out the candle, ease on to the stiff mattress, and curl back under the cool blankets. I clamp my eyes shut.

After a few silent moments, from the darkness rises the long, low wail of the siren.

Saturday, 5 October 1940

'Countess Margaret. The only grandmother ever beheaded at the Tower.'

As often as I hear Uncle's voice, it is still unfamiliar. The words seem to glide, high and then low, the tone always changing. Nothing like Mum's firm voice.

'Seventy-one years old, if you can believe it.'

I look up at him and manage an exhausted smile. We

stand together in front of the scaffold site. A paved area, hardly three feet, with a brass plate in its centre: *Site of the ancient scaffold: on this spot Queen Anne Boleyn was beheaded on the 19th May 1536.* A notice close at hand gives further names, all familiar from lessons – Queen Catherine Howard; Lady Jane Grey.

'All beheaded with an axe. Except Queen Anne, whose head was cut off with a sword. The executioner's block was known as the Ravenstone.'

Of course it was. Most executions took place on Tower Hill, and only the sensitive (mainly women, it seems) or very famous people were executed here. 'His head should be rolling on Tower Hill,' the girls at school would say about a mean teacher.

I grimace and turn away. It doesn't really bother me, though. Everywhere you look in this place, some awful thing has been done. The Tower is gloomy and horrible and savage. Here people are kept prisoner, killed, or both. *And then eaten by ravens.*

I will not live here.

'Who would have thought, even after nine centuries – older than the Vatican, the Louvre – that such a place could still hold mysteries?'

Uncle is smiling as we head towards the roost for dusk feeding. I am surprised to see him back in his uniform. ('He's been on the "sick list",' Brodie told me.) He still looks frail under the heavy cloak, his face thin behind steel-rimmed glasses. He, of course, is talking.

'On a typical day, Anna, the grounds would be crowded with members of the public, queuing to see the Armoury or the White Tower...'

Still, these are the best times, with Uncle lecturing me as if I am just another visitor – the only wartime tourist in the Tower. I gaze where he points, nod when he stops talking, smile encouragingly. He is, after all, my only family now.

I was not always so nice to Uncle. When I first arrived here, that long month ago, I could do nothing but stare at the knuckles of his hands, covered in thick black hair. He smelled like years of damp.

'But... Mr Reed—' I had said.

'"Uncle", please.'

Then, before I could stop it: 'Mother never said your name.'

'Well, she wouldn't have.' He smiled ruefully. 'Adults can be very foolish, Anna.'

'You take care of the ravens?' I asked, not wanting to hear some strange man talk about Mum being 'foolish'.

'That is one of my duties, yes. I am the Ravenmaster. Legend has it that there have always been six ravens at the Tower. Charles II himself said, *If the Tower ravens fly away, the kingdom will fall.* So you see how important it is to look after them. In fact, I could use a little help.'

'To feed them?' I said in surprise.

'We are all rationing here, Anna. The ravens get enough to survive, just like the rest of us. Ah,' he said, interrupting himself as I soon discovered is his way. Once he wandered ahead in mid-lecture, leaving me to imagine how Walter Raleigh met his end. 'Would you care to observe?'

I wanted to make an excuse, but his pace had quickened. I still felt a little light-headed, a little less than myself. When we reached the winding staircase, it was all I could do to keep my balance. Uncle noticed, slowed, and at one point reached out to steady me.

'I am just a bit tired,' I said and we continued.

Now, though, it is Uncle who is always tired; Uncle who can't make it up the stairs without a 'short breather'; Uncle who looks drained and grey and small. His speeches are still the same, though. *The Tower is important to the people of London. The ravens are important.*

I shiver, thinking about the birds, warm in all their feathers, again waiting to be fed. All except Mabel, who is alone and free.

We walk to the cages, Uncle's voice gliding on, until the words themselves are gone. If only I had a warm hat – or a fizzy pop. *Or a way out of this ghastly place.*

Uncle has fallen silent and for a terrifying moment I worry that my thoughts have become words. But he is merely observing the birds, offering here and there an understanding cluck.

Dusk feeding is difficult. The ravens fuss before returning to their cages. Late to bed, early to rise. We are lucky for the shorter days. Ravens sleep at sunset, so in the summer you must feed them at 5.30 p.m. and then return at 9 p.m. to whistle them to bed. Now, with the bombs, they must be in their cages before nightfall.

Most kids were sent to the countryside, to families, big houses and fireplaces, windows with normal blinds, a life surrounded by flying birds. I was sent here. To live with fat, squatting ravens and a gas mask that Oakes forces me to carry everywhere.

To my own cage.

Dark, swimming eyes watch me.

Raven MacDonald is already in his cage. He must be hungry. I move inside the bars, filling the water bowl (also the bath). My fingers tremble slightly. Ravens are *black*. Black feathers, black beak, black claws, black eyes. The entire head, and nearly half of the beak, is covered in thick, midnight feathers. They move around me now – ravens everywhere, sleek and guilty.

Often, if it proves too coarse, MacDonald will drop the biscuit in the water bowl to soften. He is also known, on his way by, to tug at Uncle's trouser leg, a sort of greeting. He only glares at me.

'You are safe here, you know,' Uncle says, misunderstanding my silence.

'I know.'

'You see, Anna, in order to become a Yeoman Warder,

one must serve at least twenty-two years in the armed forces.' He smiles now. 'Did you know that? We were all there, in the Great War. Now London is the Front, and we are here. Retired, maybe, but soldiers every one of us.'

I think of all the queer old weapons, axes and pokers that line the walls. Black cannons at every corner, old and useless. *Is this how you'll protect us?*

'Mum would have wanted me to have a weapon,' I say, knowing I sound like a child.

Something changes in his face.

'Your mother and I lost our brother to the Great War – he came home, but not like himself. Nerves shattered, and he died not a year later. I'm not sure how well you remember your grandmother, Anna. It was very hard on her, losing Richard like that.'

I don't remember Gran very well – she was old, shrivelled, quiet. I do remember when the war started, how angry Mum was all the time.

'I helped out as soon as I could, being the eldest,' Uncle continues. 'It was a great struggle for us all. Your mum didn't want that for you.'

I *know* Mum didn't like war – she would say things, write things: *wars are always lost*. But people *had* to go and fight. She could not be mad at that.

She was more angry at how hard life became. Even before that I had worn some of Mum's old dresses, cut and sewn to (almost) fit me. But it was the winter of the war that I was given her trousers. 'All the girls in

Kensington wear trousers and lipstick,' she said, though her smile didn't feel right. The girls at school giggled when I wore them, maybe because Mum never got me any lipstick.

And what the hell does Uncle Henry know? Clearly Mum didn't like him. And it's obvious he never came to visit me. I can't even look at him now, afraid my anger will boil over. Uncle only likes the birds because he can hobble after them. He lies about the history and the legends, the need to always keep six, just so he can cut their wings and keep them trapped here.

Mum talked about Uncle Richard, how he died when they were young. She never even mentioned Uncle Henry. Who is this strange, old, sick man?

He is watching me and leans forward. 'Are you all right, my dear?'

I am being hard-hearted. He is worried about me, that is all. In my thoughts I apologize to him. He is a lonely old man who loves the Tower. I know that he stands at the walls at night, using his secret whistle to try and call Mabel home.

'Uncle,' I say, 'Has nobody ever escaped the Tower? Truly?'

'No one has ever escaped from the Tower alone. But I suppose one prisoner did... disappear.'

'Disappear?'

'Well,' he sounds strangely pleased, 'I guess you two have something in common after all.'

I have no idea what he is talking about and can only smile weakly.

'Did you know that Yeoman Oakes is right now – maybe this very moment – writing a history of the prisoners in the Tower?'

He stares down at me expectantly.

'That sounds very interesting, Uncle.'

'Yes, well, I certainly think so. Now, you must go and ask him about the prisoner who disappeared. He can do more than tell you the story. He can *show* you. Go on, I can finish up here.'

He scatters the meat in Cora's cage, tempting her inside.

What can Yeoman Oakes show me? About a prisoner who disappeared? While I worry again that Uncle is very unwell, he is red and smiling as he ushers me across the Inner Ward to the Guard's Hall.

Oakes is not there.

With a sigh of relief, I dash back towards my room. Even the small chamber filled with spiderwebs seems a blessing. Uncle gave me a hot-water bottle earlier, which might still be warm. The wind finds me in corners, chases me round passageways. By the time I climb up the ramparts, I am beginning to feel like myself again.

Then I see Oakes.

He is walking – striding – across the Outer Ward towards Traitors' Gate. Why? Warders come and go across the bridge at the West Gate. Nobody uses Traitors' Gate, which is flooded with water and blocked by a spiked gate. Am I imagining it, or does something about him look *guilty*? He certainly isn't writing a history book.

I stop, peer down at him.

Oakes doesn't seem like one of those men who had a bad time of it in the Great War – who had their *nerves shattered*, like Uncle Richard. Something, though, is definitely *wrong* with him.

He passes the Watchman, and after some exchange the Watchman leaves. Oakes looks around, clearly checking to see if anyone has their eye on him, and then steps over the chain fence. His hat disappears as he descends.

What – into the water?

I lean over the edge of the ramparts to see. There is no water and Oakes has taken the stone stairs and marched right up to the wide span of the arch.

A man stands on the other side. I squint to see him. I can make out the chequered pattern of colour through the black bars. A tweed hat, a brown coat.

Who is he? Why is Oakes having a secret meeting with a man at Traitors' Gate? I duck behind the turret, my mind racing. Something is wrong. And why is there no water at the gate? I walked past yesterday and there was definitely water. Glinting with coins that tourists had tossed in. And the way Oakes looked around. Who could possibly be on the other side of the gate? The *portcullis*, Uncle called it, a heavy black gate with spikes. Obviously someone is visiting the Tower in secret.

To see Oakes?

I brush aside the stiffening fear. No, I can hear something… a scraping. It is a raven. Just there, not a foot away, sharpening its beak on the battlements. A feeling of shadow falls over my body. *Merlin?* Where did he come from?

Another sound. Human footsteps. I am suddenly frantic. *Oh, Merlin, you great menace. I will be caught.* It is Oakes, I know it. He is coming up the ramparts. My breath catches. *He knows. He knows I have seen him.*

A drumming sound of feet on the stairs follows me. Panting, I turn. Too fast, one foot catches the other, and I am lying on the stone.

A hand falls on my shoulder and I almost scream.

'Careful now,' comes a voice. 'Dark enough in these towers, even in the day. Up you come.'

It is Sparks, the Gaoler. He chuckles, unaware of frightening me half to death.

'Well, how are you, little miss?'

Although the Gaoler is an important person in the Tower, Sparks acts very kindly to me. He never eats at the Bloody Tower, but once we played cards in the tavern, and he let me win, happily drinking mugs of ale – 'settling the dust', he said in his deep Glasgow voice.

Sparks extends an arm, helps me to my feet. I smile as

best as I can. My knee throbs from the fall.

He takes off his blue hat, wipes his forehead. The hair that remains to him is bright white, like clumps of snow over his ears. He is the only one in the Tower of a grandfather age. He looks out over the ancient castle, red in the sunset.

'Pretty sight, isn't it?'

No sign of Oakes down there; only Merlin, his black eyes inspecting me, his head almost turned upside down.

'It is beautiful, Yeoman Sparks.'

'In 1928, at 1.30 a.m., a tidal wave swept over the wharf, filled the moat up to its gills. Worry is that a direct hit from an incendiary could flood it all again. And we'll be needing those carrots.'

It is hard to imagine the moat filled with water. The trench of earth is now an allotment of vegetables, worked daily by both men and women. *And it is always carrots.*

'I hope the moat stays dry, Yeoman Sparks.' My hands are still unsteady. 'I must go and feed the ravens. With Uncle taken ill – he needs my help, sir.'

He puts his hat back atop his glistening head. The old face, a mask of lines and wrinkles, splits into a smile.

'Those birds. Next thing we know, you'll be just like Henry, and then we'll never hear a word about the Tower that doesn't involve those bloody ravens. Come on, dear, I'll walk you back safe and sound.'

'Allow me,' comes a voice.

Standing at the end of the passage is Oakes.

'Yeoman Oakes, sir.'

He is looking at me with sharp eyes. Sparks has almost disappeared down the passage. Should I cry out? Call him back?

'What are you doing up here?'

I can think of nothing else to say – *should I just run?*

'Looking for you, sir. Uncle told me to find you. But you weren't in the hall—'

'Looking for me?'

There is no doubting that he is angry. At breakfast, Oakes is always so quiet he seems to be listening, which makes me nervous. Once he starts talking, though, I always wish he'd go back to staring at the wall. His voice is dry and cracked, as if he needs a glass of water. *Or port.*

'Yes. I have a question, sir.'

He knows. He knows I saw him.

'What is your question, Anna?'

'It's about the... man who disappeared all those years ago. The prisoner.'

'I see.' He is still looking at me, searching. 'And your uncle asked you to come to me?'

'He said you could show me something. I don't know what he meant, sir.'

'Aha.' Even as he tries to hide it, his face perks up. 'So you've been inside the Salt Tower?'

'No, sir.'

For a moment his strange look returns.

'Well, Anna. Then I'd better take you. Let you see it for yourself.'

'I should go back… to help Uncle with the ravens.'

Oakes does not even turn round. *Why is he so horrible?*

'I was beginning to worry that you had no curiosity when it comes to Tower history, Anna. I wonder how Hew Draper caught your interest.'

I can find no words. *Hew Draper? Is that the man who disappeared?*

We walk in silence across the Inner Ward.

He leads me alongside the curtain wall. I follow the blue coat and hat, always a few steps ahead. The wind is up, and in the coming night it is cold. I walk stiffly on.

A tower stands just ahead, at the end of a short bridge. The outer stone rises up before me, dark and stained. Uncle may have said this was an important building. I stare at it, fighting to bring to mind anything helpful. The bridge shines damp.

'Ah,' he says, turning a corner. 'Constable Tower. It will bring us to Salt Tower. Let's hurry now, and see it while there is still light.'

See what?

Oakes beckons me across the bridge without another

word, his cloak trailing in the wet leaves. I look up this time, staring hard at the dark stone.

I am not afraid.

We enter the tower in silence. The archway is narrow, even for me. I squeeze down the dark hall (how did Oakes manage?) and take the very steep stairs. Up and up, finally leading to a room.

All I can see are old weapons and dust. It is windy, even inside, and just as I think it, the wind picks up, echoing in the silence. We move deeper into the tower, past rooted pillars and giant arches, all smooth grey stone, the colour of nothing. Suits of armour stand to attention.

The passage continues for what seems like miles. Already I long for a roofless space. Oakes gestures for me to follow him deeper inside. I can move freely enough – I can feel my arms and legs again (and the bruise already forming on my knee).

The air is damp, heavy, the faint light giving Oakes more than one shadow.

Winged figures – angels, I guess – stare down from the walls. The endless stairs make my knee ache. Stumble-footed, I climb. The temperature drops with each step. A cough floats down on the cold air. Our steps ring in the silence.

Oakes slips through a narrow archway that opens up to the large upper room. Another stale, clammy room, with thick wooden rafters holding back the stone.

All at once I see something. Opposite the window, near the floor.

It's like nothing else I have seen in the Tower. Intricately detailed, quite beautiful, it is... *something*... carved into the wall. A drawing, or a sign. Obviously it does not belong here. It is not part of the Tower.

'Hew Draper made this. An innkeeper from Bristol, and a prisoner here a long time ago.'

Wind breathes through the room, and I step closer to the carving. The series of criss-crossing lines leads out from the centre. Is it a map of the secret tunnels and passageways of the Tower? Is this how he disappeared?

'So it's... a map?'

Oakes smiles. 'In a sense. It's a form of zodiac wheel. Beautifully done, each constellation rendered alongside the days of the week and hours of the day. All perfectly accurate.'

A map of the night sky? Why?

Before the blackout, only a few stars were ever visible in the city. Now, when I walk back from the shelter, I lose count. But I don't know the name of a single star, not one.

'How did he make these drawings, of the stars and things?'

His smile grows. 'Same way as all the others did. Using the knife he ate with.'

'How did it... help him to escape?'

He laughs, a not unpleasant laugh, his shoulders going up and down.

'Well, perhaps it did. He certainly vanished without a trace. Of Hew Draper's death, of the rest of his life – there is no record. At the time they thought it was sorcery.'

Sorcery? A small leak, quiet but steady, drips water in the corner. After another moment of expectant silence, I cough. Oakes is not a spy, or a traitor. Would a traitor really meet with someone at Traitors' Gate? I was just spooked by Merlin. And there is no secret tunnel out of the Tower. Oakes is simply a boring old man fascinated by walls.

Still, other thoughts nag at me. Oakes at breakfast, muttering about 'making peace with Hitler'.

Salt Tower is locked, and we leave by another exit, which includes even more stairs. I grip the rope tightly, wishing there was a banister for balance. But who *was* he meeting with? Warders never seem to talk to anyone except each other. That man at the gate was definitely not a Warder. *Could* he have been meeting with a spy – a German?

Oakes has marched ahead down the dark passage. There is a draught here, and the walls seem to lean in. I stop when a sudden thought strikes me. Always Oakes talks about how he hates Churchill. About peace with Hitler.

Churchill is coming. Next Sunday.

I stand fixed, staring helplessly. What if Oakes is a spy? What if he is plotting to kill the prime minister? He thinks it will end the war. He is mad... No one is safe. Anything is possible.

'But nobody knows what did happen to Hew Draper,' comes the dry voice, 'he simply vanished – into the corridors, inside the keep. Some people say he is still here somewhere.'

His voice echoes back to me.

'So please be careful, Anna. In gloomy old places like this, we sometimes see things that are not truly there.'

Sunday, 6 October 1940

For another night the raid is over. Still, I listen, each slow breath escaping in plumes. I must be certain Uncle has gone to sleep. Even after a long night in the shelter, he might trudge up the stairs to check on me.

And I will be gone.

In the dark my narrow room seems empty. But I know what is there, in the corner. The tightly pulled blanket and warm pillows. And here I stand, feeling the cold from the open door. The half loaf of bread from dinner in my pocket. My wool coat and trousers.

I am ready.

My shoes pad softly down the winding stairs, past Uncle's room. The stairwell is solid and black. Surely he is asleep by now. In silence I reach the main door. I heave it open, guide it softy closed.

Goodbye.

Cold rain hits the cobblestones. I walk alone in the darkness, my coat pulled tight. Countless windows from the huge White Tower overlook the Inner Ward. All are dark. The bombing raid may be over; the blackout is not.

You are mad, Anna Cooper. This is madness.

Another thought enters my head, another voice.

You can do this.

A crumbling wall rings the Inner Ward, and I stay as close as I can. Rain blows everywhere. Only three exits lead out of the Tower of London. All run alongside the south outer wall, and all have guards positioned throughout the night. There is no escape through any door. Ahead march tall peaks of stone, black and hard.

There is only one way.

For a moment I think I hear something, a whisper of sound. A low croak.

The ravens. Have they heard me? Those bloody birds will give me away. Even locked in their cages they are a nightmare.

Mum used to warn me, *Don't let your imagination get away from you.* Flo always said, *You are mad, Anna Cooper.* Mum is gone. Flo is gone. Lips pressed, I keep moving. It is several hours yet before the birds wake.

I have seen them for the last time.

I pause at Cradle Tower gate. Voices, definitely. Human voices, welling out of the night. Warders. A moment of panic threatens to overwhelm me. If I am caught out here...

The voices grow louder.

I rush back, crouching against the cold wall. My breathing has stopped. The rush of some distant gutter blocks out sound. They will shoot me.

You are a twelve-year-old girl. They will not shoot you.

If Oakes is planning to kill Churchill in broad daylight, he won't think twice about shooting me now.

He has already warned me - threatened me - not to tell anyone what I saw. I saw him, talking to a spy. I am sure of it.

I can't waste another thought on Oakes. On any of them.

Noiselessly, the two Yeoman Warders appear, first as huge magic-lantern shapes, then as themselves. One is Yeoman Brodie, obvious from his great size. The other is the Watchman, whose name I've clean forgotten. I wait until they disappear inside the Inner Ward, cloaks snapping behind them. Darkness swallows the passageway.

You can't turn back now.

New guards will come. Along the south wall runs a corridor leading to Develin Tower. Silently I step towards it. The entrance steps are cut high and narrow, wet from rain. I take them cautiously, trying to maintain speed. *There are no hidden passages, no secret tunnels. There is only one way.*

Climb.

Waves crash against the banks. Down there, in the glowing night, is the Thames. The Germans target the docks, every night. The fire, the heat – I can *feel* it from here. The air flurries with something like burning paper. I keep moving, breathing wildly, dodging it as best I can. Not far now, another twist of the passage and I will be at the ramparts.

Develin Tower, a squat turret at the far corner of the grounds, is hidden in shadows. Unused.

I reach up, beneath the blanked-out window. I can see nothing. A long breath. Stretching out, my fingers rub off the smoothness before finding a handhold. Not too wet. There. A narrow opening in the stone. The cold singes my fingers.

Just like a tree. You can do this. Like a tree in Hyde Park.

With a grasping hand I find the other, deeper hold, then the next, and pull myself upwards into the night. Another long breath. With a series of muffled groans, the toes of my shoes skidding, I climb.

My foot slips. I barely swallow a scream. Hanging in the darkness, I take deep gulps of black. The stones themselves seem to be listening.

Climb.

I scale upwards, reaching the final inches of the old wall and lifting myself on to the wet crown of the tower. The wind comes sharp and quick. I squeeze my hands, lumps of ice, under my armpits.

For a moment I stand completely still, scared to move.

If Flo could see me now. A brief second of satisfaction is all I allow myself.

I must escape. I must get free of this place.

Smoke curls among the ruins of East London. Many of the buildings have burned to the ground or split like exploded rocks. Small lights bloom like a sea of candles. Even this rain will never put them all out.

Smoke, fire, the reek of charred timber and melted brick reaches me.

I must get out. Another thought rises up, almost instantly. *Where can you go?*

I will go to Montreal. I will find Flo.

Hope, Mum would say with her stern look, *is a good breakfast but a bad supper.* I think again of the bread in my jacket.

Come down.

For a moment, I ignore the voice. For one thing – I don't *hear voices*. Only sometimes, when I need a little push, I imagine Flo is still with me, what she might say.

Come down.

But I take another step, the air cutting through my jacket, and look over the side of the turrets. Below, the dry vegetable garden is a drop of forty feet or more. I would never make it. The wind sings across the battlements.

Home may still be out there. Whole and safe. Or smashed like a flower vase.

A different voice now. Uncle Henry's voice.

No one escapes the Tower alone.

Taking a final look at the cold river, I make the slow descent, hands still numb, the rain driving me to the ground. I land with barely a sound. Through the stone forest of passageways I hurry to my room, hearing in Uncle's warning a sudden hope.

No one escapes the Tower alone.

Then I will need a recruit.

3

Monday, 7 October 1940

In my search for escape, I had forgotten all about
school.

Tower School, it turns out, is in the Mint, my favourite part of the castle. It feels most like a real city here.
Not that there are shops, or bakeries or clothing stores, or
anything really, but it is a long street filled with homes and
people in ties and regular hats. Kids playing with balls and
a cat sleeping in a patch of sun. And a dog, all black, that
runs around barking its head off. Young trees and potted
flowers, and even, on the small cobblestone courtyard,
shoots of grass rising between the joints.

My old school had a grass track behind the main building. Mrs Wilson said that I was the fastest twelve-year-old
she had ever seen. I know she's kind – and I know that
Flo is just as fast and she is only eleven; her name, after
all, is *Florence Swift* – but she was the games teacher and
wanted to make me like running. I always have: the wind

pushing against my face, the jolt of life.

There is no playing ground here, of course, no track or netball. Not that I can imagine playing – seven o'clock in the morning and only snatched moments of sleep. At least school is different from all the bare halls and stone ramparts; or sitting in front of the silent Green, staring at hopping birds.

The classroom has a musty smell, like clothes not quite dry on the line. *I* have dry clothes. The school has issued me a uniform, which Uncle has paid for with eleven ration coupons. A grey skirt and ankle socks. A size too big; it is very unbecoming – not what Mum would call 'from the Paris collections' – and cold. But dry, and clean.

Before Mum's accident I had only just started second form, and now I'm starting it again, though certain to have forgotten all my lessons. And how can anyone care about trigonometry when bombs are falling? *And one of the Warders might be a spy plotting to kill the prime minister.*

The teacher, Miss Breedon, sits behind a high desk, next to a blackboard framed in wood on an easel and already covered in Latin verbs. I recognize her from Sunday Chapel, when she wore a large hat. She is pretty, almost young. Her voice is soft, and the way she speaks is familiar. She reminds me of those women from the Red Cross sewing parties next door at Mrs Morgan's.

Some of the other girls I recognize too. The one with blonde hair I have seen riding her bicycle around the cobblestone alleys – even at night, with a pen torch (head-lights are banned). Girls and boys of all ages, even some babies (reception-year students) in pigtails, talking happily amongst themselves until class begins. Everybody knows each other, of course. Most are pale and thin from lack of sleep and food, with lips chapped white. Some seats are empty, and each one poses a question: evacuated? *Gone home?*

The girl who shares my two-seated desk was also at Chapel, I'm certain. She sat across from me, near the altar, her face *very* pale. I thought perhaps she'd been nervous – I was – but even now she has the pale look of someone who rarely goes into the sun. And again she wears a red ribbon in her hair.

Once morning break arrives and milk cartons are brought in for the babies, I turn to her and smile. She *is* pretty, her features small and neat. I'm sure the teacher said her name is Leslie Ballard, but, scared I'll mix it up, I don't risk it.

'Hullo,' I say instead, 'I'm called Anna.'

'Magpie.'

I blink. Why did she say that?

'Thought all the useless mouths got sent away.'

'Useless...?' I cough, at a loss for what to say. 'I was sent here.'

'So you are a vacuee? Only you've come east to do your bomb dodging?' She says this with a nasty laugh.

Vacuee. I remember the story Eileen from third form

told us. She had been evacuated to Bournemouth with her sister, and the people were so awful that after only two months they came back to London. 'Bombs are better than people,' she said.

I couldn't imagine such a thing to be true until I met Leslie Ballard.

All morning I get plenty of knowing looks, but no one else talks to me. I can hear them whispering, though, calling me 'Magpie'.

'I've never seen a ginger one before. What's all over its face?'

'Disease,' says Leslie. 'From eating all that rubbish.'

My freckles? From eating rubbish?

Brodie's son, Malcolm, who Uncle insisted would be my 'new best mate', fails to say a word to me. None of these will be likely to help me escape.

When I am called on in Latin class to answer, my voice is slow and weird.

'*Contendo* – to stretch, to aim. A sort of, ah, an exertion.'

It's as if I'd never had a conversation before. Again and again I am called on.

Why the flaming hell can't Miss Breedon just leave me alone? *I am not from the East End – so what? Why are you all so proud to be common? My mum was a journalist. I live in Maida Vale!*

In front of them all I should eat the chocolate I took from the kitchen.

Between classes Leslie walks towards me, a squat girl in tow. I free myself from the clanking seat (almost spilling the inkwell) to meet them. I am not afraid.

'Tell her, Kate.' Leslie's eyes are bright, triumphant. She reaches up, patting her hair. 'What your dad said.'

Before I can decide if I should simply walk away, Kate is speaking.

'To be vigilant. To look out for people who don't belong, even girls. It's in a government booklet. People who seem *weird*. People like you, Magpie, who might be German spies.'

'I am not—'

'Don't tell the enemy anything. Don't *talk* to the enemy.'

Now I do walk away, and their giggling follows me. A beastly voice calls out, 'Send her home'. Girls at my old school could be mean – making jokes about me having freckles or not having a father – but they weren't this rotten. Leslie's head should be rolling on Tower Hill.

Already the day feels a week long.

Why did Mum take that stupid bus? What was she thinking? She has left me here, alone, with a sick uncle and mean commoners. How could she?

It is a short walk to the loo, at least, even if the battlements are freezing. Of course now it is raining, any trace of the sunny morning gone. And I've forgotten my umbrella.

Orrk. Orrk.

A raven on the Green, its dead-black eyes following me. Raven Edgar, I am sure.

'Move,' I say harshly.

The bird breaks into a reluctant trot.

The loo is a room of cramped, grey stone. I shiver as I grab the pull chain and hurry back outside. Just as I reach the school (Edgar jeers from a stone perch), I feel a headache nagging at me. I am especially frightened by headaches. When Mum had her migraines, it was horrible – 'savage', she called it. She would have to lie still on the bed, no sound or lights, with brown paper soaked in vinegar across her temples.

If I can make it through the final class, Uncle will have aspirin. And I will tell him how I can never step foot in this horrible school again.

'You new?'

A boy is gazing at me. He has bushy, dark hair and a slightly too large head – which I recognize as belonging to the boy who sits two in front of me, just to the left. His eyes are red like everyone's from the hanging smoke and dust.

He is standing alone in the rain. *Why are these kids so bloody mean?* I squint my eyes at him.

'Don't call me Magpie—'

'Did you see the Heinkels dive and hit the wharf last

night? They look like cigars, but they drop breadbaskets. You need sand for those, not water.'

He speaks so rapidly I have trouble following him. The accent is still unfamiliar. At least he isn't being mean. I let out a breath I didn't realize I was holding.

'Yes,' I say, offering a slow smile. 'I'm called Anna. Anna Cooper. Who are you?'

'Me? Bomb expert,' he says, shaking my hand. 'Timothy Squire.'

The rain is cold and slanting and we are not quite under the cover of the ledge. I feel my hair growing heavy in the damp.

'Bomb expert?'

'You don't believe me?' He cocks an eyebrow, which only draws attention to the expanse of his head above. 'You think I run and hide in the shelter with the old folks? Come on then. Tomorrow afternoon, when the tide's out, me and the lads'll go down to Pier Head. Easy enough to find an incendiary in the mud. All you do is unscrew the cap, remove the phosphorous into a paper, right? Then chuck it on the bonfire and watch it go up.'

Timothy Squire talks and talks, the wind whisking his hair. And in those few moments I learn many things. Chiefly, that he doesn't care where I'm from or why I'm here. Also, and at length, that he escapes the Tower. He meets up with friends, goes bomb-hunting, plays street cricket, explores wreckage. A possible recruit, indeed.

'Stray cats are everywhere – all fat and lazy because

high explosives wrecked the sewers and now there's too many rats to eat.'

He talks too of 'fireweed', the pink flowers that grow and blossom in the ashes of the city. And I know it is true. There is something... a smell... of air and bright wind. He doesn't smell like stone and darkness, but of freedom – of the world. We are still standing, defenceless, in the rain.

'Can you show me?'

''Course.'

He offers me half a biscuit, pushing the other half into his mouth. I take the biscuit and hold it in my hand. All I have eaten today are eggs from the chickens and some hollow wartime bread.

'You'll love it. Bombs leave all kinds of mess,' he says, chewing. 'Dead horses. Horse guts all over the road this morning.'

Love it? I nod anyway. *He can get me out of here.*

A silent moment surfaces, sudden and abrupt, and I rack my thoughts for a way to ask him: *When can we go?* I am too slow.

'What're you here for then?'

'I look after the ravens,' I say, my voice strangely proud.

'Ravens? Not for long.'

'What?'

'They got rid of all the animals at the zoo. Evacuated, or...' He runs a thumb across his throat in a sickening gesture. 'Can't feed 'em. Same at the aquarium. Drained the whole thing, shot the manatees. You know, sea cows.'

'They did not! My uncle told me—'

'You going to feed them? Pay to heat the tanks and all that?'

'They don't *shoot* them.'

'Better than letting them starve, right?'

He flicks some crumbs from his sleeve.

'Why are you rolling your eyes?' he asks.

'I'm not.'

'What did your uncle say then?'

'A plan is in place,' I say, 'to protect the animals.'

'Yeah. Like I told you.'

The sickening gesture again.

'Well, *I* protect the ravens now. So they will be safe.'

Suddenly Miss Breedon appears under a black umbrella at the other end of the corridor. I thrust my hand behind my back, my fist closed round the biscuit.

'Timothy Squire. Get back into the classroom this moment.' Her gaze flicks to me. 'I am not sure what kind of institution you attended previous to joining us, Miss Cooper, but here at the Tower School we arrive on time for our lessons. Come, both of you, out of the rain, quickly.'

Wednesday, 9 October 1940

'A strange man?'

I swallow, hard, and try again.

'A man. Not at the Gatehouse. By Traitors' Gate.'

Uncle turns to me, a glow in his eyes. 'You know that Traitors' Gate is a water gate? Prisoners had to enter on a barge, passing under the heads of executed criminals displayed on London Bridge. Queen Anne Boleyn—'

'Yes, but when the tide is out.'

It was something Timothy Squire had mentioned. Surely that is how the man was able to walk up to the gate.

'Well, dear, Yeoman Oakes *was* a Company Sergeant Major,' Uncle answers, ignoring my question about the tides, 'in conversation with all sorts – Scots Guards, Royal Highlanders. Likely it was an off-duty soldier. And those Royal Highlanders are some of the strangest folks you'll ever meet.'

I nod, unsure how to continue. What can I possibly say? That I saw Oakes talking to a strange man through the portcullis? *That is the truth.* That he could be planning to kill the prime minister? What would Uncle – what would anyone – say to that?

'Come on, you lot.'

Uncle gives his whistle and dumps the bowl into the cage. In horror I realize my stomach is growling – I *am* hungry, but not for bloodsoaked biscuits. The chance of having Welsh rarebit for dinner, however, is slim.

Uncle gestures to the birds with a smile. 'You know where the word "ravenous" comes from?'

I watch them tear and jab for as long as I can.

This week could not get any worse. The girls still

whisper, giggle. At least I had the satisfaction of enjoying a leisurely few minutes eating the biscuit under Leslie's watchful gaze. Timothy Squire – who couldn't stop talking on Monday afternoon – didn't say a word yesterday. Not once has his giant head turned round in its seat. He promised to take me out of here.

Why did I tell Timothy Squire that I would protect the ravens?

If the Tower ravens leave, Britain will fall.

Grip arrives – a black flicker, and he is there – to collect his meal, as Uncle Henry predicted. I think I notice a smile of relief, though. Surely Uncle fears Grip will go in search of Mabel. *She is an example for us all.*

'Uncle. Don't the ravens... want to be with the other ravens? The free ones?'

He gives me a look. 'When did you last see a raven, Anna?'

I shrug. 'All the time. On rubbish day.'

He laughs, filling up MacDonald's bowl. 'Those are crows, my dear. It's a hundred years or more since a wild raven has been seen in London.'

Really? I thought these ones were just bigger – well fed and flightless, but the same bird.

'What happened to the wild ones?'

'Shot, mostly.' He is frowning, and after a moment I frown too. 'Ravens have always been held in suspicion. The dark arts, and that sort of thing. On battlefields, they flocked to the dead soldiers. As you may have heard me say already, they are extremely sophisticated birds. They soon discovered that when groups of men in armour meet in a field, it means dinner is coming.

'So they would follow the armies and simply wait around. *We* misunderstood, and thought the ravens were an ill omen. We assumed *they* brought the death and destruction.'

When Uncle talks of battlefields and slaughter, I think of Leslie and her giggling friends. But some part of me shivers at the echo of Oakes's words. *Their big dinner is coming.*

'So how do the ravens protect us?'

Uncle gives a patient smile. I am reminded again how different he is from Mum. It's not just his voice. Mum always had a quick temper, and she could be horribly brisk when she was doing something else, something *important*. Uncle is kind, his green eyes soft, apologetic. And once I saw him after breakfast reading Agatha Christie, which Mum would never have done.

He thinks I will stay here, with him and the birds. A sudden swell of pity rises up, but Uncle doesn't notice me.

'Since Charles II, the ravens have been here, serving as sentinels. They were kept there, on the top of the White Tower, and whenever they spotted something that didn't seem quite right, they would croak warnings.'

Aren't they warning us now?

'It's true, Anna. They warned of the Dutch attack, and when Colonel Blood tried to steal the Crown jewels. And who do you think it was that alerted the Warders to Guy Fawkes and his gang?'

'So the ravens guard the Crown jewels?'

'My dear Anna, the ravens *are* the Crown jewels.'

Saturday, 12 October 1940

If it was guns that kept the ravens out of London, they won't be coming back now. If the war continues, Raven Mabel is gone for good.

I have fed the birds and have hours I could spend on the wet bench before my lunch. I used to love the outdoors. At home, usually at night, I would open the back door and take huge lungfuls of air, as if being inside was the same as being underwater. Nothing felt better, even when it was cold out. But this is *too* cold.

I should go the library. The room is dry and almost warm.

Mum would have loved it there. She was always reading. Not the papers – where her own writing went – but big, heavy books, books with boring old covers, without pictures or drawings or any colour at all. She was always arranging and rearranging them in the bookcase, and anyway they were too heavy to carry anywhere. Sometimes, too, there were old *Tatler* magazines and she would sit flipping the thin pages, making sounds under her breath. Except in the last days, when she sat knitting and listening for the silent radio to crackle to life with news.

The moment I rise from the bench, imagining a dry roof, Timothy Squire appears on the Green. He is walking right towards me. There is nowhere for me to go. I sit back down.

He just saw you get up.

Committed, I lean back and gaze around coolly. The sky above is dull with its usual clouds and fog. This, on the other hand, is unusual. All week he has said nothing to me, even when I approached him after class. It is because of the time Miss Breedon yelled at us, I'm sure. I suppose Timothy Squire thinks Miss Breedon is scarier than bombs.

I sit as still as I can. Sometimes – like the time on Speech Day with Flo – I laugh without meaning to and carry on making strange noises. And I can feel it beginning now.

As his footsteps reach me, I look up and see him.

'I want to show you something,' Timothy Squire says, standing right before the bench.

'OK.' My voice is a little breathless, but he is already marching away.

Now? Are we leaving now? I have not said goodbye to Uncle. *I have not warned him about Oakes.*

Smells of roasting potatoes waft towards us, making it hard to focus. Surely we can eat before we go? It is clear we are going deeper into the Tower. If he is taking me to Salt Tower...

Timothy Squire is leading me inside the barracks. Up

a broad flight of stairs I follow him to a flat. It is large –
there even seems to be an upstairs. *Is this his home?*

I stare around, entranced. It is warm, swept – like a
proper house. Made of stone, of course, though the air
doesn't seem so heavy and stale. A light switch sticks out
from a circle of cut paper. Two glaring eyes above, a stub
of a moustache below. Written around it are the words:
Save fuel. Snap Off Hitler's nose.

A voice calls from the back.

Timothy Squire is waiting in a small room with oak
panelling on the walls. First I notice all the books – though
not quite *books*. Thick and sturdy, they are nevertheless
comics: *Adventure, Wizard, Hotspur, Rover.* Is this what
he wants to show me – a comic book? Mum didn't let me
have comic books after my eighth birthday.

'Here,' he says, and begins rummaging around in a thin
closet.

In the silence I glance back at the door. *His parents.*
Will they be upset to see me here, unannounced? I should
have told Uncle I was coming here.

With a happy sigh, Timothy Squire picks up something.
He turns, all smiles. It has a beautiful silver polish, with a
little fin on the end.

'Bloody hell.' I take a step back. 'Timothy Squire...
That's a—'

'Incendiary. Like you wanted to see.'

A clock ticks on a high shelf.

'Don't worry,' he says. 'Moment I found it, I unscrewed

the cap. It's a dud. Polishes up nice, though, doesn't it?'

'Yes, but – what I meant was – could you show me bombs and things *outside* of the Tower?'

He tucks the smooth shell away again under a mound of jumpers. I see, for a moment, other glittering objects. *What else does he have in there? Shrapnel? Landmines?*

''Course,' he says to my continued silence. 'What do you want to see?'

'The docks,' I blurt out. 'And the incendiaries around there. Can we go tonight?'

Timothy Squire shrugs, then shakes his great head. 'No. Not tonight. Tomorrow – tomorrow morning after Chapel.'

I frown. That's when Churchill comes. *What if Oakes tries to kill him?* What can I do? Uncle doesn't believe me – he won't have a bad word said against his great friend Oakes.

'Tomorrow morning,' I agree.

I can't worry about Oakes or Churchill, about the ravens or the kingdom. Tomorrow morning I will be on a ship, headed to my new home in Montreal with Flo.

Tomorrow I will be free at last.

Cold leaks up from the stone.

When is sleep more important than safety? I am now

curled atop three blankets on the shelter floor, gas mask in my hands. Around me various parents and children are scattered across similar blankets. Uncle is here, on his usual bench, and Oakes and Yeoman Brodie in chairs. Oakes looks tired – old and tired and hardly like a spy. *He is a Warder, and a firewatcher at St Paul's.*

Warders are everywhere, at every gate. Churchill will be safe. They will all be safe. If there is a spy, he will be caught.

A woman I don't recognize, with a child in her arms, sits on the single bunk. Above them is a sign, written out in big letters.

ONCE A PERSON HAS GONE INTO A RECOGNIZED SHELTER THEY MUST REMAIN IN THAT SHELTER UNTIL THE ALL CLEAR SOUNDS. IN EXCEPTIONAL CIRCUMSTANCES THE MALE OF THE HOUSEHOLD MAY BE PERMITTED TO LEAVE THE SHELTER WITH THE APPROVAL OF THE WARDEN.

Usually the kids play 'Air Raid', which involves running up and down, shrieking, and knocking things over. Tonight, though, everyone is quiet, even the young child.

At home we had a Blitz drill. I would run and close the shutters and bolt the doors. Mum would hurry to fill the bath and the sinks with water. We assembled in the sitting room, opposite the fireplace. Even before the war Mum always drew the front drapes. We would run up for the mattress, and drag it bouncing down the stairs.

If bombing was close, we had to squeeze under the table. Any closer, and we gathered all the blankets and took the wet garden path out to the cold Anderson shelter.

Uncle has risen from his chair, and he kneels down close to me. *Did I say something, cry out?*

'It'll be over soon, love.'

He is right. When I wake up it will be tomorrow. And Timothy Squire will help me get to the harbour and find a ship. And then everything will change. I will be headed far away from here. Montreal. Quiet nights, happy dreams, proper food. No ravens, no legends, no bombs.

Uncle is kind. I will write to him from Montreal and thank him. I will write to him and explain it all.

I would have liked to have seen home again. I have not thought of home in days. The blue door, almost grey at the edges. Pints of milk outside, the newspaper folded on top. My room, a front room, with views of the street – of people and horses and motor cars. Red geraniums on the window sill. The untidy bookshelves. Lavender-scented soap.

What will it be like now? It won't be the same as Florence's family, who covered rooms carefully in dust-sheets, and packed silverware and pottery away in newspaper. The house will be as it was, maybe with a layer or two of dust.

Will someone look after it? The police, or the fire-watchers, old Mrs Morgan next door? Some day, I will find out.

One more night. I pull my knees closer. As the low, distant sound continues, I feel my eyes closing. When the sound dries up, I have fallen asleep.

I dream of red geraniums.

II

THE LION AND THE RIVER

Long dark months of trials and tribulations
lie before us. Not only great danger, but many
misfortunes, many shortcomings, many mistakes,
many disappointments will surely be our lot. Death
and sorrow will be the companions of our journey;
hardship our garment; constancy and valour our
only shield.

– Churchill, speech to the House of Commons, 8
October 1940

4

Sunday, 13 October 1940

Not until eight minutes to four in the morning did the All Clear sound. That wonderful, flat, steady sound. Then two hours in my bed. For once I am happy to have slept in my jumper. It is far too cold to even imagine undressing. And now it is all over.

I have made it.

I wash my face and hands in the freezing water from the bucket (*not* lavender scented), immediately towelling myself dry and warm. This morning I put on a little of the cold cream – nearly half gone already – before lacing up my shoes and leaving the room.

Today is the thirteenth of October. It didn't even occur to me how perfect it all is – *of course* today is the day I escape. The best gift of all. I swiftly take the long twisting stairs to the Stone Kitchen. I will not miss them, or the old thick rope that burns my hands as I descend.

Uncle is up and cheerful for the dawn feeding.

'Do you see? Equal chunks, four ounces.'

He gestures to a square of meat, about the size of his palm, and begins to chop it into smaller chunks. The cleaver thuds on the wood.

'Now, see this?'

I glance up, nodding. He is holding an egg, slightly brown and spotted.

'Every other day. A boiled egg. Shell on.' His slow voice is firm. 'These are for tomorrow.'

Tomorrow. I am almost sad to hear him say it. He will have to feed the birds alone tomorrow. He will have to find someone else to listen to his stories. *He will miss me.*

I am wary of the next preparation, though, which also occurs every other day – the bloodsoaked biscuits. First they look like the dry Melba toast that Mum always had at tea, but then they are pulped into red oblivion with a potato masher.

What a thing to be doing on *this* morning. It suddenly dawns on me that Uncle might know that it is my birthday – maybe Mum once told him, and he remembered. I am not hopeful. It is not important, not now. *Proof that I will* not *be missed.*

I watch as carefully as I can. As ever, his movements are deliberate, considered. Uncle manages not to get any mess on his suit and tie.

'I know it is hard, when there is so little to eat, not to resent the ravens. But you should see their usual diet. A rabbit every month – with the fur, of course, the fur is good for them. And plenty of table scraps.'

The idea of table scraps makes my stomach rumble. Their meal prepared, Uncle pulls on his black leather gloves. While he always wears gloves, today he has something else in his hands, something different.

'No,' I say before I can stop myself.

He laughs, not trying to hide the large gleaming scissors.

'Don't worry, my dear. Every three months we do this.'

We climb into the weak light and up the stone steps to the Tower Green. Other birds, small, bright birds, sing as we pass. I study the trees, but Mabel is not perched in the low branches. She has not returned to say goodbye.

No one else is up and about. At this hour, the Tower is only open to the gate guards and the milkman. There is no sign of Oakes or the strange man.

'Here,' Uncle says as we arrive, opening the cage of Raven Edgar. 'Watch.'

I take quick breaths, the air still heavy with soot from last night's raid.

Uncle picks up the raven – not without some difficulty, Edgar is a bad-tempered bird at the best of times – and he flutters like a chicken and swoops round the cage until Uncle is forced to grip him by the beak.

Maybe Edgar knows what is coming. His eyes are sharp and wide open. Ravens *look* at you, recognize you, in a way that cats and dogs never could. The eyes are *not* black, I realize. They have dark brown irises. Human eyes.

I am not too squeamish to watch Uncle cut some feathers. *The birds are happy here. Special.* Uncle holds the black bird in his right hand – Mum was left-handed too – and calmly snips at the end of the wing. Small black tufts float to the grass. The raven bites at his gloves, but with no real force. Uncle grins.

'Just like a haircut.'

I smile back, absently pulling my copper ponytail. Edgar marches away, his dignity seemingly intact.

I close the cage door and again hoist the bucket. We move on down the roost.

It is hard to look at Raven Grip now. It always reminds me of Mabel – which is mad because *they all look exactly the same.* Little black goblin creatures, teetering back and forth. I remember Uncle's other words, spoken days ago now. 'Ravens mate for life. Paired ravens mimic each other.' Will Grip disappear too, go off in search of Mabel?

I will him to do so. *Go, be free.*

'Not too much trouble, was that dear?'

'Not at all, Uncle.'

Now I am grinning. Feeding is over and it is time for Chapel. I am done with the birds. And I am meeting Timothy Squire.

The Chaplain, standing proudly in front of the grey Chapel, beams at the Tower residents. Even the NAAFI girls from the canteen are here. Clouds hang heavy and the air is white with mist. Sunday weather. But this is not a regular Sunday.

A bugle sounds and the Warders' parade marches into view. Today the uniforms are red and gold, with white ruffs at their necks and short black hats – like travelling into Mr Fenwick's history textbook. Medals and ribbons are worn across the chest, and they all seem to carry large spears over their shoulders. Sir Claud Jacob himself, the Constable of the Tower, is here. We watch the Warders turn and march, and then follow them inside the Chapel.

I sit in my usual wooden pew, listening to the whispering and shuffling. My stomach growls after the measly cereal and no egg (not even a brown and spotted one). Many other uniforms are here too – the Scots Guard, the Grenadiers, the Women's Royal Airforce in their blue wool. Everyone has come: Miss Breedon, in a flowery dress; Sparks, sitting quietly by himself near the pillar; Yeoman Brodie, his funny red uniform pressing against his wide chest. Even Leslie, with a tall, horsey-looking mum.

Timothy Squire, though, I do not see.

A boy that I think for a second might be him turns his face slightly – it is not. Timothy Squire's father, I have discovered from cautious questioning of Uncle, is the curator at the Armouries Museum – a rather boring man who I once helped pack boxes. I do not see him either.

I'm not bothered. At breakfast, I raced through the washing up. Yeoman Cecil's eyes were wide – he may not have completely finished his cereal – but everything was dumped with a heavy splash into the sink. Moments later I was dashing down the stairwell. *He will come.*

Organ music begins, slow and heavy. I pick up the books – *New English Hymnal, Book of Common Prayer* – and put them down again. Light floods in from the large windows all around. Still, it is cold. But I shiver with excitement. The service, Sung Matins, is brief. Although the choir is small – two boys, three men, and six girls – their voices are sweet. I am so happy I even smile at horrible Leslie and her horsey mum.

Instead of the Chaplain giving his sermon, a Warder stands and reads from a paper in a stilted voice.

'Now that winter is approaching and the blackout is daily becoming earlier, it is essential to look carefully and improve the blackout. There are many windows and doorways still showing light…'

He drones on. The first thing I will do once I arrive at my new home in Montreal is tear any bloody curtains from the windows.

We sing a nice hymn, and it is a frenzy of giggling voices before the crowd reappears outside the Parade Grounds. I recognize some of the Wives – and, with a shock of distaste, Headmaster Brownbill. Raven Cora, a thin branch in her beak, marches past in her most military bearing, and carries it off rather well. No sign yet of Timothy Squire. Again, I think I see him except it is an older boy, who looks quickly away.

Then, through the autumn fog, a black car arrives and slows to a halt in front of the barracks. Timothy Squire is not here.

But Mr Churchill is.

A man, massive in black, leaning on a stick, beams up at us: a heavy, puckered face above a bow tie. He is old – maybe as old as Gran when she died. While people call him 'the British lion', he looks to me like a great black rooster. *Or am I spending too much time around birds?* His voice we all know from the radio, lisping and growling, though I cannot make out any words at this distance.

He is not alone. A woman – his wife? – and some men in uniform, gas masks over their shoulders, walk alongside. Press photographers swarm round them. Sir Claud Jacob comes forth to meet the new arrivals. My eyes strain to see if Timothy Squire is close by. Where is he?

No announcement is made. Instead, the group breaks off, the rest of us trailing behind. Where are they going? The White Tower, to address us from the heights of the castle?

It seems they are first giving Mr Churchill a tour of the

grounds. I follow, near the back of the large group. Uncle walks nearby, with Oakes as usual by his side. Oakes's face is tight, strange.

We are not taking the usual route. First, the prime minister is lead east to the Officers' Mess, and then to the North Bastion. Sir Claud is pointing out the damage. Workers stand idly by, watching the procession. All hammering is to been stopped for the duration of Mr Churchill's visit, as he can't stand the noise.

The Constable includes nothing from the regular tour (Uncle has given it to me enough times that I could do it myself), talking instead about the structure itself. Standing outside Traitors' Gate, the prime minister is told how the wall dates from the 1200s, and has thirteen defensive towers and a fifty-foot curtain wall.

Oakes met with a strange man right here. A sudden fear floods me, and I squint through the portcullis. No one is there. And water fills the entrance.

Sir Claud nods towards the prime minister. 'An extraordinary fortress.'

'Not "extraordinary",' Mr Churchill says with a shake of his head. 'All fortresses have walls. Rather, "remarkable".'

At this all the Warders laugh, even the Constable, and the crowd moves onward. I watch Oakes. His face is deathly pale.

Instead of listing the many illustrious prisoners once held within the Guards' Chambers, Sir Claud spends much time detailing the damage to the roof. Why are the photographers taking so many pictures of the other towers – the untouched Brick Tower and Flint Tower and the Brass Mount?

Then Mr Churchill is led into the White Tower, past the pillars and gloomy vaults, and through the Banqueting Hall where Anne Boleyn was tried and sentenced to death. None of that is spoken.

Then a question occurs to me; lost beside my need to escape, it now seems vital.

Why has Churchill come?

The tour comes to a solemn stop at the tavern, and I find myself inside. Other students are present too, a dark-haired girl about my age, and a squat boy standing before his proud father. Not the giant forehead of Timothy Squire. Voices mutter and talk. We are like sardines in a barrel.

The prime minister and his men are offered pints, and the great man takes a sip with obvious satisfaction. Somehow I am quite close. Uncle is a little further behind but Oakes, I realize, is standing *right beside* Churchill.

He would never try something in front of all these people. Would he? I cast my eyes around for the strange man in the tweed hat. He is not here. Churchill is pointing out something on the atlas.

Now I stare at Oakes, unable to look away. His face is unsteady, his lips moving silently. I have been wrong. He *is* going to do something, I am sure of it. Pressed in on all sides by the crowd, I cannot move to stop him.

'When will the war be over, Mr Prime Minister?'

Oakes's words crash over the other voices.

I blink in surprise. People shift and glance downward.

'Can we have the truth for once? Your photographers seem to have missed most of the damage. When will this war be over?'

Eyes still focused on the map, Churchill answers, unsmiling. 'When our task is done.'

'What task, exactly?'

'Of cleansing Europe from the Nazi pestilence and saving the world from a new Dark Age. If Hitler cannot destroy us, we will surely destroy him, and all his gang, and all their works.'

'Will any civilians still be left, here or in Europe? We are carrying out the same bombing plan as Hitler.'

'The only thing I have in common with Herr Hitler is a horror of whistling. You won't be whistling for us, will you, sir?'

Mr Churchill looks away from the atlas. All at once, he appears to see me, and a way to dispense with Oakes's conversation.

'And what is your position here, my dear?'

My voice is scratchy. They are all listening: Leslie, always touching and patting her hair, mean Miss Breedon always calling on me, and horrible Kate, probably on the lookout for spies.

'I... I look after the birds, sir. I'm the assistant Ravenmaster.'

He repeats 'Ravenmaster' vaguely, as if his mind is elsewhere. My voice goes mechanically on, filling the uncomfortable silence.

'Since Charles II the ravens have been here. If the Tower ravens leave, the kingdom will fall.'

A sound comes from behind me – a great intake of breath from Uncle, or a mocking hiss from Leslie?

Churchill, though, is silent. For another brief moment the great face turns towards me, and whatever he sees there makes him smile. Then Churchill lifts his glass.

'And a great thing it is you do here, dear. Good for morale, good for the country. Hitler's eagles are no match for Britain's ravens.'

A loud cheer echoes through the room and a camera flashblub fires off. I don't laugh along with the others. I don't think of the girls, giggling and saying 'Magpie' and 'rubbish eater' to each other. I don't think anything. I find Uncle's face and he smiles weakly.

'What if they come here?'

The return of Oakes's voice is a shock.

As the prime minister straightens his beaming face does not change. He gestures to the knives behind the bar.

'You appear to be well equipped. A bare bodkin for

every hand. If the Hun is to come, they will come. You can always take one with you.'

Everything is clear to me as we exit the pub. If the crowd was not so tight, I might have fallen. *Oakes is right.* The photographs of the undamaged towers. Uncle's old stories. The desperation. It is not Churchill I should be worried about. No spy is coming to kill the prime minister.

We are losing the war. Hitler is coming to kill us all.

'Where were you?'

Timothy Squire looks up at me. Even he can't ignore me when I'm talking directly to him. He can play dumb, though.

'What?'

'This morning – at Chapel. You were supposed to meet me.'

'Oh. I was out.'

'"Out"?' I say in disbelief. *Forget it.* Most of the afternoon has passed away. 'Well, let's go.'

'What?'

'Remember? The docks,' I say to his confusion. I don't even have time to relish his struggle to find words. 'Come on. We'll have a look around, find some shrapnel. Get outside.'

I start walking, my bag heavy at my side. I should have put on my hat and trousers. It is cold and I am hatless and barelegged. But not suspicious.

I turn back when I realize he's not following.

'What are you doing? Let's go.'

He is staring at me. I thought the temptation of shrapnel could not fail. I try again.

'Uncle wants me to get some fish for the ravens.'

'I can't. I mean, the market's almost shut – Anna, it's nearly dinner time!'

I turn and look him in the face. '*You can't?* I thought you went out all the time. You weren't lying, were you?'

His face turns suddenly red, but then he shrugs. 'Of course not. I mean, do you want to go?'

I smile my best smile. 'Yes. Let's go.'

'All right, all right. Don't lose your wool.'

As we reach the West Gate the guard in the Gatehouse looks up, his eyes never leaving mine. I hand over my ID card.

'Ah, Miss Cooper. Where are you setting off to?'

'Setting off?' I try to laugh. It sounds high and odd. 'Me? Nowhere. The bag is for the fish.'

Timothy Squire must sense trouble, because he steps forward. 'Hullo, Mr Thorne. We're just going down to Billingsgate for Mr Reed. Get some kippers for his birds.'

'Yes,' I say, trying to find my voice. 'The ravens are very sophisticated birds. My uncle – Mr Reed – has told us to be as quick as we can.'

The guard narrows his eyes. 'I know Henry's not feeling so well these days – and he does love those birds... but Yeoman Oakes has asked me to make sure Anna stays inside the Tower—'

'It's just for a minute, Mr Thorne, sir. Could grab a mackerel for yourself, if you'd like?'

And just like that we're walking across the bridge.

I am free.

Men in black homburg hats and long coats crowd past. No young men, of course – only the old ones are left. Among them move women in berets and high heels, some with elbow-length gloves and fine furs. Glamorous, even if all their eyes are tired. Mum had said people were making do with last year's coats.

'Look at them all.'

I almost expect my voice to sound higher now, released from the stone walls and shadows. The air, too, seems warmer.

Everyone looks quite smart: beautiful greens and creamy whites, splashes of blue and bursts of yellow. Heads are held high, proud, hurrying to and from bus stops and Tube stations, passing florists and flag sellers, peering at the charred ruins of the night's raid. It is *exciting* to be outside.

'Let's make tracks,' Timothy Squire says, and I agree – Oakes may not be a spy, but he has clearly forbidden me to leave the Tower. *And he is always watching.* I'm not some prisoner in his book.

The haste of the city is contagious, and we move rapidly ahead. Some are not moving at all. A fireman, weary and blistered, screams at two staring women who are standing on the hose. Many of the flats have collapsed inward. A queue snakes outside a phone box. I see no blossoming fireweed.

As we walk queer feelings overtake me: that I should know what that heap of bricks is – what it *was*. Every morning on my way to feed the ravens I see this view from the ramparts. Yet I have no memory of the old landscape. A block of flats?

It doesn't matter. I am free.

'Before we go to the market – I was wondering, can we see the docks? Before it gets dark.'

He nods absently, clearly looking for some piece of exploded metal.

We shift direction, now heading east. Streets are roped off. Unexploded bombs? Men in steel Civil Defence helmets try to marshal people, to send them home; there are too many. Some stand and point at the heaps of bricks, several feet high. Others trudge past under bags and sacks, carrying their goods.

'Why didn't you come to see Churchill?'

Timothy Squire glances at me, shrugs.

'Everyone was there.'

As he starts on some explanation I'm not listening. I can hear nothing above the sudden roar in my ears, as if a bomb had just landed on the opposite block, without warning or sirens, without even a plane passing over... it is only a bus. A normal bus, on its route through the city.

Mum.

The bus, full to bursting, squeezes round the fallen bricks. Tired faces are visible through the blast netting at the windows.

Mum's last day was on a bus like that. It is strange. I always thought of her, elegant in her dress and hat, reading the early papers in her Tube seat. I can see her, folding the paper, and at Holborn Station stepping off the train and out into the day.

In my mind I see the shelter with my headmaster and the WVS woman, that endless night, the growing hollow dread that life was about to change forever.

I stop, staring, as the bus heaves past us. The bus is wrong. I don't know why, but I *know* it is.

It is all wrong.

'Magpie. Look at this.'

I turn, absently. I have been standing in a daze, as if someone has knocked me on the head. Timothy Squire is showing me something. He is back to his old self. He doesn't notice my sadness, doesn't notice me. Just talking, talking. *And he called me Magpie!*

'It's huge!'

'Yes,' I say.

I stop thinking about Mum, about what name Timothy Squire calls me, and focus on where I am. I can only let myself think of one thing: escape.

Already we have reached the docks. The wharf is a massive concrete sprawl the size of several playing fields. Black shadows of cranes are everywhere. I look wildly for a great ship, waiting for me, bound for Montreal. I have seen many, from the Tower, that were surely headed for Canada. Up close, however, it is harder to tell.

The docks lurch with people. It is not at all how I imagined it. So different from the canals of home, the bright-coloured houseboats of Little Venice.

'They always target here,' Timothy Squire says, his voice serious. 'The target is the guide.'

For once, I know what he means. The docks are the gateway between Britain and the world: bringing in war materials, food, help. If you bomb the docks, the ships get destroyed *and* the fires help the planes orient themselves.

I have heard many stories – areas bombed so heavily that buried fires still burn. We push closer, dodging a rough hole in the cement. *How deeply buried?* Then Timothy Squire laughs, and his voice resumes its mischievous tone.

'When the bombs hit in the summer, rats poured out of those buildings like waves. Thousands of them!'

I turn in horror, expecting to see a tide of rodents swelling round us. He goes on talking, about flaming barges filled with coconuts, which burned for days, nothing could put them out. In the brief second where he draws a breath, I speak.

'What are those ships for?'

I point past a distant column of smoke, rising from behind the river. From here I can see that it climbs miles high, darker than the dark clouds.

He laughs. 'You've never been down here before?'

'I have,' I say defensively. 'I just don't know a lot about the docks, or what's where.'

'Never could have guessed,' he says. 'That smell, yeah? What's that like to you?'

I inhale deeply, playing along. The air is pungent, heavy.

'Nutmeg,' I say. 'Like Christmas.'

Timothy Squire nods. 'Spice docks.'

Other smells too. Sulphur and char. He then proceeds to tell me all about the warehouses, the wharves, the nearby rail lines and power stations. Further east, the Woolwich Arsenal, the Ford Motor Works, the Beckton Gas Works. Not a word about where the passenger ships are docked.

I *have* been here before, even visited the Tower. I was very young, and hardly remember anything about it. One thing I do remember, though, is the river, up close. It was not like this, thick with ships and smoke.

In my mind, the water is quiet and calm, leading out to the North Sea. It seemed impossible that it could have harmed Father. Impossible that it could have killed him. *Then why are you so afraid?*

'When Dunkirk was on, you should have seen it,'

comes Timothy Squire's voice. 'Everything that could float. Destroyers, paddle steamers, sloops. More ladders than you ever saw, hanging over the sides of each ship. Everyone down here was making ladders.

'Then the barges came, and the small boats, red, blue, yellow – fishermen and crabbers, some of them never been off the river. Headed to France to pick up the army. Mad, isn't it? At second tide they all left – it was about as dark as it gets in summer, but you could see them clear, just a block of boats, filling the river. Still, no lights or any noise, hoping the Germans wouldn't know they were coming.

'It was like the Spanish Armada,' he says, breathless. 'They brought back thousands – tens of thousands – of soldiers. The Germans kept on bombing them as they headed home. Everywhere ships burning and sinking. Imagine it.'

Clumps of people fill the alleys. Refugees maybe, or poor children who had been evacuated and drifted back to London. Yeoman Brodie said there are more refugees every day: French, Czech, Polish, Dutch. Everyone looks lost, strange.

Everywhere ships burning and sinking.

The flats are small, poorly made. The abandoned ones

look the same as those with people in the windows. We pass a large black man, and some people not speaking English. A new, unnameable smell hangs heavy in the cold air.

'We're near the coloured quarter, Jews and Indians too.'

I nod. I know that once the war started, aliens had to move away from the coast – had they all come here? I remember too what Mum said about 'class feeling'. *During war, we're all the same.* We still don't *look* the same, though. Mum always said not to be narrow-minded.

Lonely fires burn themselves out. It is amazing how slowly all the clearing up is done.

'It's nice to be out,' I say instead.

Timothy Squire gives me an odd look, perhaps guessing my lie, and I immediately ask, 'So you spent your whole life here?'

''Course.'

'Do you like it?'

'Like it? Sure.' He frowns. 'Not Frederick. Or Malcolm – or anyone from class. Or any of the Warders, the old bores. It's brilliant, though. And with Elsie and the NAAFI girls here now...'

'Elsie?'

But he is already walking down the wharf.

'Come on,' he says.

We get free of the docks, and once again I recognize things: the post office, newspaper and cigarette shops. I can smell something delicious – the smell of frying.

'Look at this,' he says in awe, standing over a clump of silver. He gestures for me to pick it up.

'What is it?'

'Come on,' he says. 'You're a bright spark, have a guess. Go on. Give it a go. It's why we've come.'

Not certain he isn't teasing me, I reach down and grab the clump of metal. Cold, and only jagged on one edge, it's some piece of shrapnel; I'm not listening to the lengthy explanation. The silver reminds of something else, something I am foolish enough to have forgotten until now. Even if I could sneak off to the docks and find a ship bound for Montreal, how would I pay for it?

And when I arrive in Canada, where will I go? Ask around until I find someone who knows Florence Swift from Maida Vale?

The North Sea is dangerous. It killed Father.

I offer the metal to Timothy Squire and, after a moment of fake protest, he pockets it.

As we march down the narrow streets, past the small ruins of terraced houses and the great ruins of factories, the sound of the lapping river recedes. I clutch my bag tightly, my eyes turning back to the waiting ships.

'So what bomb was it that got you?'

'What?'

'Well, you were bombed out, weren't you? High explosive?'

I shake my head. Can't we talk about anything else?

'You don't know? Your own house, and you don't know?'

He seems truly shocked.

'Maybe now,' I say, refusing to look up, to look west. 'Maybe now it is in ruins. When I came here, the house was fine.'

'Then what are you doing here?'

He is looking at me like I have wings or something.

'My mum died,' I say. My throat is hot. 'On a bus. I don't know what type of bloody bomb it was, all right? She died, and my father drowned when I was five. My house was fine, but I couldn't go on living there alone, could I? My only family left is my uncle, so *that's* what I'm doing here.'

'Did you get the furniture out? Or was all your stuff spoiled?'

'Why would Uncle take the furniture out? If the house is still standing when the war is over I shall want all the furniture exactly where it was.'

It is late. No matter what arrangement the Warders have – and they seem to have an arrangement with everyone – the fish market looks closed. It *smells* open, though. Then a woman walks past – shiny face and tall hat – a bag in her hands. The scent of fish tickles my nose.

I hang back, shivering, while Timothy Squire strides

ahead. I wonder if I should try to change into my trousers, or at least put on my wool coat. What would Timothy Squire think? *He would wonder why I am carrying all my clothes to the fish market.*

Before I can decide what to do, he has returned with a newspaper-wrapped fish. How do I not eat this myself?

'We should get back,' I say. 'We'll be late.'

Timothy Squire smiles. 'I know. This was your idea.'

But our pace has quickened. The air is cold, with sand blowing around us from torn sandbags. I am aware of eyes watching us. The refugees from the docks?

What time is it? None of the church clocks tell the right time any more. Entry to the Tower is banned after 7 p.m.

'Well? What will we do? We won't make it back in time.'

He is still smiling, as if inspecting some newly discovered piece of shrapnel. I am sure someone is following us. Two kids, carrying food through the streets at night? *By the docks.*

'Don't worry,' he says. 'There's a drainpipe.'

A drainpipe? I hurry ahead at a jog, with Timothy Squire stubbornly walking behind me.

We have to climb a drainpipe? In almost darkness? And over the wall? A far more dangerous route than the hand-holds on the side of the Develin Tower. What will Uncle say? Oh, and if someone sees us – in the dark – and thinks we are spies? Parachutists?

I walk even faster, willing the Tower to appear. *It will*

be worse if someone catches us before we get there. In the dim light I can make out four towers, rising like great teeth. There it is! I couldn't have imagined being happy to see the great pile of stone. And thank God the guard is still visible at his post.

He does not even look angry. *He was waiting for us.*

Of course he was. He wouldn't lock up with us still out there. Another truth rushes in, and my face feels hot.

Timothy Squire was teasing me. *There is no drainpipe.*

Mr Thorne nods and Timothy Squire, handing him a wrapped bundle, has the nerve to smile back.

5

Hitler swooped down on us again last night. Never before did I think of night as early, middle, and late. It used to be one blank stretch.

Yesterday I awoke in the late night, a Wife's words in my head. *I can't bear the night. I can't bear the night.* When I tugged free a wax earplug, the bombs roared. Moments later, the siren called us all into the shelter.

Once I arrived at breakfast, I discovered how dreadful the news was. Balham Station, not far from Clapham, took a direct hit and six hundred people suffocated when the bomb trapped them inside. As always, Mr Cecil referred to it as 'an incident' and Oakes went on a long rant about the evils of war.

Malcolm, Mr Brodie's often-mentioned but rarely seen son, appeared at breakfast. Despite Uncle and Mr Brodie talking about our great friendship, the boy looked at me precisely zero times. Apparently, I learn from Uncle, Malcolm has a great love for diamonds and jewels.

At school, Headmaster Brownbill called me into his office. The foul man slurped his tea and delivered a long speech, of which I will forever remember each ridiculous word.

'You like to write, don't you, Anna? Some of the teachers say that you even write during lessons. That is not good because you will never learn what they are teaching you if you do not pay attention' – I am missing lessons *now*, I wanted to shout – 'but I understand. I like to write as well, you see. So I have a plan for you. Stop writing in class – really, you must learn along with your classmates – but keep writing after school.

'Write down everything, how you feel, what you think. And then don't show it to anybody, not your teachers or your uncle. Write only for you. Write only for your eyes.'

Setting his cup down he jostled it, hot liquid tipping over the rim.

'Sorry,' he muttered to the cup.

'While I was in the trenches, I wrote a letter every day that I could. You should do the same. Keep every letter you write and store them away. Somewhere safe, mind you. You never know how they may help you. Do you understand me, Anna?'

When I saw Headmaster Brownbill later in the hall, he was still stern and cruel, and he growled at me to walk faster to class.

The rest of the school day was equally horrid. Lessons about the war effort, the agencies, the committees, and the abbreviations. Girls calling me Magpie and rubbish eater. The end seemed like it would never come and staying awake was nearly impossible.

'If no student has any questions, we can conclude for the day.'

No student did.

All in all, a terrible day. Now, from under the hard bunk, I take out my diary. I *will* write, but not because the headmaster told me to.

I should write to Flo and ask her address – tell her I'm coming. All I can think of is the Balham disaster, and my own time with Mum down in the Underground. The only toilet, up in the booking hall, was closed at night despite the need of it. There was a heavy stench of too many bodies and overflowing latrine buckets. Some people just used the rail tracks. Children were running, playing hide-and-seek on the (switched-off) escalators, darting beneath signs on the walls: *Coughs and sneezes spread diseases.*

Trains, before they came in, were stopped in the tunnel so policemen could march down the platform and gently (for the most part) push in any overhanging feet or arms. Then the train came rattling along. People slept heavily, through the terrific noise and the blazing electric light, bundled together on the cold floor, under the clouds of mosquitoes.

I tuck the diary back under the bed and close my eyes.

The press photographers have returned. Churchill is not with them, no tour of the damage is given. They are led straight to the roost, and Uncle offers me an apologetic smile.

He steps forward, clearing his throat. He seems to be addressing me as much as the press.

'Since Charles II the ravens have been here. If the Tower ravens leave, the kingdom of Britain will fall.'

Cameras whoosh and clunk, the flashbulbs firing off.

'As you can see, they are safe and well looked after.'

He does not mention that there are always six ravens. *That one of them is gone.* A few more flashes, which Raven MacDonald clearly finds annoying. He hops away. Photographs, we are always reminded, are never allowed at the Tower during the war.

Uncle gives a soft smile, and accompanies the press back to the entrance. I will finish the dusk feeding alone.

One raven returns ahead of the others. I can tell it is MacDonald from the slinking walk. Up close it is obvious. Hard to believe I once thought they all looked the same. I close MacDonald in his cage and whistle for Grip. Grip is the largest, and he has the thickest beak and most prominent ruff of feathers at his neck. He is last to be rounded up for the night.

He tilts his head at me, scoots away in two-footed

jumps, looks at me again. I feel certain – I *am* certain – that such displays are for me to see. If I wasn't here, he wouldn't do it. Are you telling me something, Grip? Or just trying to avoid your curfew?

Ravens are not robins. They are not cute; they don't sing happily or hop in excitement. You don't want to hold one, to feel the softness of its belly. At home, it was always my job to fill the feeder, a *much* more pleasant task than here. And though I never got close enough to touch one, a robin's belly must be the softest thing there is.

If there are still robins in this city, they keep away from here.

I whistle again as Grip makes his slow way towards me. The ravens are not like pets either. Nothing like Mrs Morgan's old terrier. Uncle is always talking about how sophisticated, how *smart* the ravens are. He even says that they recognize him. They *do* look at him differently – differently from how they look at me anyway; then again, I haven't been feeding them for years like he has.

Something changes, something in the air, and we both look up at the sky. The rain has not come, and it is slightly warmer beneath the clouds. Something else is coming.

In that moment, the unthinkable becomes necessary. Grip, so hostile to humans, does not protest when I grasp him firmly by the wings and heave him off the ground. When I remember that I must hold his beak closed, he is already inside the cage.

'Sorry!' I yell as I run, the first flashes of gunfire lighting the sky.

I hurry down the long stairs into the White Tower basement, the siren wailing. The warden, an irritating girl called Violet, lets me in, too shaken to be suspicious.

All the questions I was prepared to answer must now seem pointless. 'Who are you?' 'Are you in the right shelter?' 'Where is your uncle?' Violet asks no questions. My name is not ticked off a list.

I move swiftly inside. Dark shapes occupy the corners, shapes that turn out to be old weapons, cannons and pikes. A hurricane lantern sits in the middle of the narrow room. No dartboards or newspapers down here, though an electric radiator provides heat. It is not heat we need.

An explosion.

Despite being deep below the ground, surrounded by thick stone, the shelter itself lifts and moves, like a barge in the choppy Thames. With a horrible crunching sound the steel door pushes inwards and outwards with the suction. The heat is immense. No one stands near the door; no one speaks.

The White Tower is being bombed.

Another blast and everyone huddles together. Maybe Uncle is safe in the Casemates. Timothy Squire too – even he is not mad enough to wander out during a raid.

'My house!' A woman suddenly stands. 'It's got my house.'

'All right,' says Violet, her voice nervous. She tries to start a song.

'Shut it.' Another voice – Headmaster Brownbill? – shouts her down. 'We've got enough noise without you.'

Silence again, until voices rise up, whispers becoming conversations, impossible to ignore.

'I wish you would all stop talking.'

'My house. I know it. It's got my house.'

I blink behind my hands. I see Father's face now, not serious but smiling, a full wide smile. *I can do this.*

The slow hours pass.

The All Clear sounds. The man – it *is* Headmaster Brownbill – is the first to leave, not even testing the shelter door before shouldering it open. His choked sobs seem to echo across the entire city.

I stumble into the near darkness. The White Tower still stands, proud and tall amid the smoke. The rest of the Tower has not been so lucky.

Walking among the shrapnel, the red-hot lumps of metal, I keep my eyes on my feet. Timothy Squire is *fine*; he always is. Uncle, too. I will see him in the morning. *Mere hours from now.* I talk to no one, look at no one, and soon I reach the top of the stairs and the door to my room, and fall on to the hard bed.

'With high explosives, *always* count the bangs. If the noise gets louder, the next one is coming your way. Then you lie down fast and raise your chest off the ground. That way the vibration won't crush all your ribs. Keep your arms over your eyes too because glass will be flying everywhere.'

After another horrid day of school, it is difficult to follow these new lessons. Timothy Squire and I sit in the study along the Casemates, the flats and rooms built into the Tower walls. The Inner Ward is an unholy mess, so all the students have come here after class to play the few games stacked inside the trunk.

Some of the babies play hide-and-seek. They don't even go to the good spots, down the long corridors or into the towers, but just crouch behind a wall. Even in here, the heavy smell of smoke finds us. Monopoly is the only game I know, so Timothy Squire and I are playing that. I am quite hopeless. Florence would get so mad if I didn't understand some game she wanted to play. Timothy Squire just laughs.

I find myself liking him and his slightly too large head. He acts as though life hasn't been cut in two. As if this new life, with its bombs and shelters, could be filled with laughter and fun. 'A bloody good sort,' Flo would say.

I wonder, for a moment, if Timothy Squire is falling in love with me. Flo told me all about it when annoying

Edward fell in love with her. I wonder if he will try and kiss me? Perhaps I will let him, and then we will talk all the time – even at school – and he will help me feed the birds every day. He bites his fingernails, though, which is disgusting.

'Magpie. It's your turn.'

'I know.'

It is difficult to imagine him outside of these walls – in Hyde Park, or at the café Mum used to like by the canal. But he does not fit with these stones and the towers. I take my last sip of the weak tea.

'You don't have brothers and sisters?' I ask.

'I had a sister once,' he says, 'when I was little. She was older. Gone when I was three.'

'I'm sorry.'

'I don't really remember. Mum talks about it, though.'

Well, at least he still has his mother and father. And all of his *things*.

I shake my head, concentrating on the board. My little silver dog is now surrounded by spaces owned by Timothy Squire. When did he manage to get all those? *This game is stupid.*

I squeeze the looped handle of the empty teacup.

'Why don't you say anything in class?'

'Like what?'

'I don't know. Anything.'

'It's class.'

'But you grew up with them, right? Don't you like any of them?'

He finally looks up at me. He seems several years older under his checked cap.

'I like your birds.'

'Do you?'

We sit in a happy silence. *So what if he is a little boastful?* He likes to have fun, and I have fun with him. *And he likes the ravens.*

'You never told me,' Timothy Squire says, 'why you wanted to go to the docks. You don't care about the explosives.'

'I wanted to escape.'

'What do you mean?'

'I mean,' I say, not sure at all what I mean, 'I thought I needed to get away from here.'

He is looking at me. 'Not any more?'

I shrug. It is strange to be back in the Tower. *I was outside, I was free.* I keep thinking about the docks. Or a train – a train to the countryside.

My eyes wander to the window and the remaining sunlight. As if it were a day sunny with the promise that the sirens will never sound again.

'Want to go and look at the river?'

He gives a great shrug of his own. 'I see the river every day.'

I stand, straightening my top. I am suddenly very happy the cold weather made me change into trousers after school. I do wish I had some Vinolia soap, though.

'Come on,' I say. 'You've never seen this view.'

The shine in his eyes startles me.

'How did you get up here?'

'Same as now.' I gesture to the handholds below, trying to dim my smile and steady my breathing. *Much easier the second time.*

A huge barrage balloon has been set up over the White Tower. Much larger and more otherworldly from up here, it sways and glitters in the cold air. Taut black cables anchor it to the earth. Somehow this grey whale protects us from bombs.

Despite all his grousing – 'I'm dead, absolutely dead' – Timothy Squire doesn't seem winded. He takes a large step forward, peering over the edge like an explorer on a peak. Not afraid of heights then.

'You can see everything.'

He keeps looking, the city spread out before us, the strange balloon behind. This time I allow the thrill of the climb its full moment.

'We have to come back up here during a raid,' he says, now sounding breathless.

Tower Bridge is up, two great destroyers passing down river, the sun shining over it all. The smell of the spice docks travels on the wind. An hour at least before the dusk feeding.

I wipe my face with the back of my hand. Although it

feels quite warm, I am glad I had Mum's old trousers for the climb. Imagine if the horrible girls saw me in trousers, what they would say – worse than 'spy'. Timothy, it seems, notices nothing different.

While he stares across London, I look out at the sprawling Tower below. From here it isn't quite so daunting. The ancient walls look chalky, almost soft. A thousand years it has stood here, since William the Conqueror made it his home. None of Uncle's many lessons come back to me. Nevertheless, it is an amazing sight. *The juice is worth the squeeze*, as Flo's father would say. The raid damage is mainly along the North Bastion walls, now blasted black. Stone spills into the passage, the smooth turrets crunched by the bombs. The rest of the Tower rises solid, strong. Our fate is not decided yet.

I see only one blue coat, heading in the direction of the White Tower. And a black smudge, perched motionless on the bench. *My bench*. Likely Raven Edgar extending his territory.

This morning I checked with renewed hope to see if Mabel had returned, maybe waiting in front of the roost, ready to have breakfast with Grip. Surely she misses him, misses her home. But Mabel has not come back.

What is she telling me?

Holding my hair back against the wind, I turn to the south. Several women are working in the allotments. One stops digging for a moment, standing full in the sun. I remember sunbathing with Flo in her garden the August before the war; the soft grass, the slow afternoons. The woman below resumes her work. The distant cluck of hens can be heard.

A far cry from Maida Vale. The broad streets lined with trees, the winding canal teeming with coloured houseboats, the bustle and excitement of Paddington Station, taking people to Wales, Bristol, Penzance.

'Spitfires,' calls Timothy Squire.

While it has been weeks since I've bothered to look up at the droning sound, Timothy Squire acts as though it's his first sight of planes in formation.

'This place kicks,' says the upturned face.

I smile, but can't hold it for long. Was that the two o'clock bell? It didn't quite sound like the barracks clock. Was it a church bell, from the city?

I am acting mad. Church bells have been banned since the summer. Every Londoner knows the signal and even Timothy Squire wouldn't scoff at it. If the church bells ring, the invasion has begun. All the noises – bombs, fire, planes – are preferable to the tumbling notes of church bells. When the church bells ring, Hitler has come.

'I have to feed the ravens,' I say to the still upturned face, and abruptly begin the steep descent.

I understand, as I land on the battlements undiscovered, something I first thought after the Balham disaster. It is not the Tower that is the prison. It is the war.

I also realize that the letter I wrote, telling Flo I am coming, is still pressed inside my diary.

'Edgar!'

I have never seen him so agitated at morning feed. Uncle doesn't seem to notice – or think too much of it. Last night's raid has made them stranger than ever. Anxious, fluttering, restless. 'Migration patterns,' Uncle says, though I don't understand what he means. The birds can't fly.

'Do you know the legend of King Arthur?'

I nod, trying to hide the coming frown.

'Yes?' Uncle says, and I am embarrassed at how his face instantly shines. 'What does the legend say?'

'That King Arthur will return, some day, as a raven. So you should never harm one.'

'Good girl,' he says, and for a moment I think he will reach out a gloved hand and pat me on the shoulder. He does not.

Uncle shoos Cora into her cage and I watch her skip right back out. She is calling, croaking loudly. She never acts like this – and the others are just as bad, Grip in particular.

Kraa, accompanied by much hopping, on both feet, up and down. Uncle's expression does not change. It is likely the cold as the autumn descends into winter. Or is it the passing gulls?

MacDonald is not in his cage. The door is open, but he hasn't returned. I don't see him anywhere – and then I do.

Fear seizes me, dark and cold.

In the shallow ditch by the southern corner of the White Tower, his heavy body is twisted at an angle. Ruined and broken, motionless. It is several minutes, in the weak dusk light, with Uncle calling me back, before I find Raven MacDonald's head.

I can make no other thoughts come.

The ravens protect the Tower. Without them, the kingdom will fall.

I burst through the Gatehouse doors, rushing past the startled Watchman, and bound up the stairs, Oakes's laughing face filling my thoughts.

'You!'

My voice cracks.

Oakes is reading a heavy leather book.

'Anna.' He looks up, smiling but cautious. 'Can I help you?'

The Watchman, who followed me inside, takes his swift leave.

'It was you.'

My voice bounces from the walls.

Oakes closes his book, leaving a finger in the pages. 'What is it?'

'I saw you! At the gate. You hate Churchill, you hate

England, and you hate the ravens.'

'Anna.' He lets his book close. 'What has happened?'

I know it, looking at him. He *does* hate them – he called them the real Beefeaters because they steal his food. And he's jealous Uncle spends so much time with them. *He killed poor MacDonald. He cut off his head. I know it was him.*

He stands, looming over me. 'Who have you been talking to?'

'I know what you did. And I will prove it.'

Thursday 17 October 1940

The siren is half an hour early and each night is colder than the last. I have to clench my teeth to stop them chattering.

He cut off MacDonald's head. Why? Is this another warning? So I won't tell Uncle? Maybe it wasn't Oakes at all – maybe it was someone else?

I have put Oakes from my mind. I do not smile at him at breakfast but I will not say sorry either. *Someone* did this, and if it wasn't him… I don't know. *How could anyone be so wicked?* To murder an innocent bird. No one else seems to care. They have graver worries.

Hitler is going to invade.

Nobody bothers with the shelters any more unless the bombing is close. Tonight, we are free to try and ignore it. Soon the sky through the window is a flickering red, and then a glaring white leads the way. Often the colours swirl together and I watch the reds and blues and oranges transform the wall. No need for a torch. And anyway mine appears to have run out of batteries. (It is near impossible to get new ones.) Or frozen dead.

I should take my workbook from underneath the bed. We've been kicked in the head with homework. The idea of returning to class fills me with loathing. I have pages and pages of notes to study. The book was more than half filled before Miss Breedon's lengthy additions. At this rate I will run afoul of the paper ration.

Instead I reach for my diary. It is also nearly full. I have not written in it, not a word, since I was brought here. But often I flip through the crowded pages, turning towards earlier entries.

Friday
Today we practised hiding underneath our desks. Which is awkward for most of us – and mean Helen Jones is just too fat to fit.

I skip ahead several pages, turning back when my eyes latch on to a word.

Wednesday
I hope Mum was not unhappy with Father before he drowned. I know it seems a queer thing to worry about – but I do hope that in those last days they did not fight

*or argue. That for some reason would be the greatest
sadness.*

I shouldn't have turned back the pages, of course. Though
Mum rarely talked of Father, that didn't mean she was
angry with him. Only that his memory made her sad.

I can only think of him in that photograph, sitting at
the kitchen table with Mum and me. Not quite handsome
– his ears stick out a bit *too* much – with light hair, and an
almost serious look. The hint of a smile, maybe, at his lips.
(Who likes to have their picture taken, anyway?)

A loud crash returns me to the present. I was so obviously tired at the dusk feeding that Uncle offered to put
the ravens to bed on his own tonight. Tired from the
school day, of course – how many kings are there in the
Old Testament? – not because I am too sad at the loss of
MacDonald.

I put the diary back under the bed with the workbook
and gas mask, taking out the wax earplugs Uncle gave
me. (Mum always had cotton-wool plugs, which are far
more comfortable.) I lie back, the sound muffled, and
stare round the room, trying to ignore the horrid pang of
hunger that never quite goes away.

In the darkness I don't see the empty room, the bare
window sill. I see the desk in Mum's study, the pens and
pencils, the make-up cases, the yellow wrappers from
those hard candies. When I finally close my eyes, they are
still there.

Another crash wakes me.

I slide out from under the pile of blankets, which now includes the rug – it is far too cold otherwise – and move through the dark. Uncle will expect me to be asleep. He will be listening to the radio, so I can easily sneak past his room and down to the Stone Kitchen. It is a not-so-secret secret between us that the biscuits are hidden behind the great suit of armour.

I open my door and leave it slightly ajar. Let the mouse, who has definitely returned, escape again. Cold air immediately grabs me but I shrug it off. I am not going far. Just a biscuit and then back to bed; hopefully a few more hours' sleep before the dawn.

Slipping down the stairs, I ease up before reaching Uncle's door. Seeing no light from underneath the crack, I breathe easier. He is asleep.

My foot misses the next stair. *No. I can hear people talking.*

It is Oakes's voice, coming from Uncle's room, though his tone is somehow different. I risk a step closer to the door. Uncle is arguing with Oakes. I can make out their words.

'What if something happens?'

'*Something* could happen to any of us, at any time.'

'You are ill, Henry.'

'My thoughts are clear. This is not a discussion.'

There is a silence and then Uncle speaks again, his voice softer.

'She can never know.'

The air in the stairwell is like ice. I am certain that Oakes has left the room through the back door until he speaks.

'Never? Is that in the interest of the girl?'

What girl? Me? I have forgotten all about my hunger.

As I inch forward another step, the voices cease. Have they gone into another room? What can I never know? He is angry that I interrupted his writing. *You accused him of being a spy and murdering a raven.*

I let another long minute pass; no sound comes from behind the door. Only the quiet ticking of a clock. Slowly I retreat up the stairs and pull my own door softly shut.

I sit in the darkness, eyes wide, certain of the truth.

They were talking about Mum.

Uncle is lying to me. They are all lying to me.

Hope has tricked me enough. The walls, the tunnels, the docks: every possible escape is blocked. I can't go to Montreal; I can't go home. If Hitler invades, nowhere in the kingdom will be safe.

I must stay. Protect the ravens, like I told Timothy Squire, like I promised Uncle. I must stay, in the Tower, with its mean girls and traitors and bombs. I must stay and find out the truth about Mum.

III

THE RAVENS AND
THE RUINS

Your Courage, Your Cheerfulness, Your Resolution
will Bring Us Victory.

– Ministry of Information, poster

6

Friday, 18 October 1940

Of all the rotten classmates, Timothy Squire is the rottenest.

School work is impossible when you are always tired: eyes dry, hands slow, mind drifting. Timothy Squire still never acknowledges me in class.

Leslie, who was beastly – all eye-rolling and hostile laughter – seems to have changed her mind about me being a spy. Even though she keeps calling me Magpie, she doesn't say it in the same mean way. Her laugh, too, is still nasty, but now it is directed elsewhere. Sometimes at stout Kate, who sends cross looks back at us.

Now Leslie turns to me between classes and tells me all sorts of things. 'You can still get anything you want in the city,' she says. 'You just have to talk to the right people.' Just *imagine*, someone being able to get hot chocolate and scones with cream.

Leslie is full of dreadful stories too. 'When the night

clubs get bombed, and everyone is running and screaming in a panic, pickpockets and thieves go to work. Sometimes,' she leans in cautiously, 'they take fingers.'

'Fingers?' The desk creaks as I pull away. 'Why?'

She rolls her eyes at my innocence. 'Magpie, you can sell *anything* on the black market.'

Nobody would accuse her of being a Sunshine Susie. Many people talk about the black market, and it sounds like a dreadful place – filled with cheats and crooks and bloody fingers. Is this where you get the hot chocolate?

How she hears all this, I can't imagine. Leslie knows all about the pilots too – the day boys and the night fighters – and talks about how brave they are. While it occurs to me that she would find Timothy Squire *fascinating*, for some reason I don't mention it.

Why does no one speak to him?

Miss Breedon returns and silence with her.

Leslie is a great desk partner, and far more interesting than the lessons. Flo would *love* her. I can't imagine these things happening in Montreal. She must be so *bored*.

Today we have more gas-mask drills, and we wear the masks through history class. They smell dark and rubbery and the strap pinches my ears, and the eye-pieces instantly begin to fog up.

'Great, now I look just like those stupid birds,' comes Leslie's blurred voice. With a long black beak and rounded eyes. She is not wrong. *She could be Cora's cousin.*

Before class ends, she nudges my elbow and, when I

look, makes the loudest croaking noise through her mask. Even Timothy Squire turns round, his grey eyes wide with surprise, and I laugh even louder.

'Sorry if we were a bit hard on you,' Leslie says. 'When you first came, I mean.'

'It's all right,' I say.

'We don't get vacuees coming to us. You're our first, Magpie.'

I learn a lot from her. We often sit, the hour before dusk, on the low wall. Kate is never there. (She's probably at home, crying like a watering cart.) Leslie says things are different now. Before the war, kids in the Tower were normal enough – they went to the cinema, rode bikes, ate Marmite sandwiches and ices.

'What do you think of... him?' I gesture vaguely as we leave the school. Leslie knows who I mean.

'Timothy Squire? You're the only one who can stand talking to him.'

'Oh. Why?'

'Because you're new.'

That doesn't answer my question, but for some reason I don't want to ask again. Leslie has been completely lovely. She doesn't even sound like she's from the East End, not like Nell or Timothy Squire. She seems almost fond of me now. The ravens, however, Leslie has not grown fond of. Maybe it's because of all the gas-mask drills.

'You must hate it. Being around those awful birds,' she says as we pass by the Green, a long day of memorizing the names of committees and agencies now behind us.

I shrug, but Leslie won't leave it.

'What? You like them?'

'They're not so bad.'

'Just look at it.' She comes to a stop, points. 'If you died, it would eat off your face, just like that. Pluck out your eyes and swallow them.'

'Raven Cora?'

My disbelief is matched only by hers.

'Giving it a name doesn't make it a girl, dummy. It's still vermin. Why your uncle is allowed to keep them here is beyond me.'

I shrug again, too tired to argue, as Cora turns towards me, listening. Across the ramparts the setting sun stretches her shadow. Two black eyes shine no light back at me.

To others, they are a symbol of hope. And if I can help the ravens, keep them happy, keep them here, people will not lose hope.

If the Tower ravens leave, the kingdom will fall.

'Why don't you ever talk to Timothy Squire?'

Leslie answers in a mocking, sing-song voice. 'Timothy Squire is a dirty old liar.'

She laughs, an old joke.

When Leslie and I part ways under the afternoon sky, I

exhale loudly. A crashing headache is coming. Is he a liar? A loud croak wrests my attention back to the gathering ravens. They appear much more sinister as a group. *Uncle would likely have some explanation for that.*

'I'll be back to feed you lot in an hour.'

Uncle finishes the crossword before starting the fire with the paper – *The Times*, not the *Evening Standard*. Whatever passed between Uncle and Mum stops him from even reading her old newspaper. In my first week here, I thought he was worried that I might stumble upon her obituary, as the notices are now staggered to avoid specific information about bomb strikes – which night, on which street – that might help Hitler measure his accuracy. Still there is never a trace of the paper. The fire barely gets hotter.

'Another tea?' Uncle holds up the pot. 'I think I may even have a chocolate or two if you fancy. A shop on Cartwright Street had some in today.'

He pours the weak tea. 'And you're enjoying school? Brodie tells me how you and Malcolm get along.'

I nod. *Famously.*

'Miss Breedon speaks quite well of you – a perfect lamb, she says – and tells me you're fitting in nicely.'

'School is fine, thanks.' *A perfect lamb?* 'Uncle?'

'Yes, dear?'

I don't know what to say, or how to say it, with his kind eyes on me. But I must.

'Uncle. Why... why did you never come to see us?'

'You must not remember, dear,' he says smoothly. 'I visited you, in Warwick Avenue. We had tea in the kitchen with your mother, much like we are having now. I was still in Palestine then, though I came to London whenever I could. Your mum was always happy to see me.'

'But she never did.'

Now there is something – a stiffening in his cheeks.

'Well, adults can be very silly—'

'Did you and Mum have a row?'

'Anna, your mother was a dear lady.'

'Then why did she hate you?'

Uncle has turned white, his face emptied of all colour. 'Your mother didn't hate a single thing in this world. There are just some things that are... *impossible* for some people to understand.'

'What do you mean?'

'Your mother and I had a disagreement, Anna. It just made sense for everyone if we... stayed out of each other's lives.'

'Because of my father?'

'Your father had already died, Anna. Your mum didn't want my help – didn't need my help.'

'But... you are my uncle.' I don't mean for it to sound like a question and I can see that it wounds him. 'What happened—'

'Don't worry about all that, dear. Plenty of time for the business of adults. You are twelve years old.'

'Thirteen,' I say quietly.

He gives me a confused look.

'It was my birthday, the thirteenth of October, the day of the prime minister's visit.'

He gives a sad smile. 'I am sorry, my dear. I *had* noticed... something. You do seem older. Wiser.'

He closes his eyes for a moment. Then he stands and limps over to the stack of cold firewood, adding a single log.

'Enjoy your tea, dear. I will see you after lessons.'

Uncle moves slowly, hiding the fire's glow, as he leaves the room.

Saturday, 19 October 1940

The first thing I noticed when I was brought here is how misty it is. From the river, Uncle said. It seemed yet another barrier, a castle bordered with fog. Again it is misty – and smoke-stung eyes make it hard to be sure – but I would see if Timothy Squire was on the Green.

Again he has not come.

Everything else is ready. When Yeoman Cecil offered to buy and prepare the meat, I assured him that Uncle had left the task to me.

'He showed me again and again, sir, how to chop the meat *just so*.'

Hopefully the guard at the gate will be as easy to convince. Touch wood and don't look round.

First, of course, Timothy Squire will have to show up. 'Two ticks,' he said. I have been waiting for nearly half an hour, and the afternoon sun offers little warmth. If he does not arrive soon, someone will see me standing by the West Gate and tell Uncle, or Oakes. The girls, luckily, will be in the study.

Nothing happens. From the tavern, I can hear the BBC playing 'Tipperary'. Earlier it was Beethoven, which I preferred. For some reason I'm reminded of Mrs Morgan next door, pottering around the small garden, saying 'when I had my figure'.

Once again I think of the chest of drawers at home, stuffed with shirts I almost never wore. My blue dress with the Peter Pan collar. And my riding coat, hanging in the wardrobe.

I gaze up at the barracks. Is Timothy Squire asleep in there? It seems queer to me, even after being here so long, that most of the towers and turrets are plain houses on the inside.

Finally, Timothy Squire appears on the Parade Grounds. 'Magpie.'

We walk to the Gatehouse, the guard watching us approach. Not Mr Thorne today. The guard will listen to me. I *am* the junior Ravenmaster, a Tower resident. Oakes does not dictate my coming and going. I take a long breath, steady my nerves.

The guard simply waves us through. I do not turn to see Timothy Squire's grin. *Everyone knows everyone here.*

As ever, people stream across Tower Bridge to the City. Not as many as usual, though. And quite a few are smoke-blackened firemen. At the foot of every lamp post are sandbags, some torn and burst. Bombs fell close last night.

Horses and carts rumble by on the way to the market. You can smell the apples from the end of the bridge.

'So, why the birds anyway?'

Timothy Squire doesn't like it when I go quiet for too long. *Like he does at school.*

'What do you mean?'

'What's so interesting about some birds? Dad says they used to have all kinds of brilliant animals here – elephants and polar bears. Even had a Lion Tower. Filled it with lions. Now we only have the birds.'

'You know the stories,' I say, glancing at the winding street to my left. Weston Street? I wish I had my bicycle; I could speed down the hills, keeping my eyes skinned for missing paving stones. 'You've lived your whole life here.'

'It's Yeoman Reed who tells all the stories. Nobody else really knows them.'

'The ravens of the Tower?' I say in disbelief. 'They've been here since Charles II. Attracted by the smell of traitors' corpses. Even after the executions stopped, the birds stayed.'

I can think of few other facts – *some live as long as*

forty – but the image of the corpse is enough to make him smile.

'Eating traitors, huh? I've only seen them eating that slop you give them at night.'

Does Timothy Squire really not know about the ravens? About the history of the Tower – his home? Does he really watch me feed them? From his window?

'The ravens protect the Tower, according to legend. If they fly away the kingdom will fall. If you'd been there when the press photographers came, you would have seen all the pictures they took of MacDonald. I bet the papers were full of him.'

Poor MacDonald.

Timothy Squire doesn't appear to grasp the seriousness of it all.

'Why fly away?' He shrugs. 'Got all the food they want here.'

'There's more to life than food.'

We arrive at the vast covered stalls of Borough Market. No wonder we saw so few people on our way; they are *all* here. We are taken up by the crowd and pushed steadily inside. Above, the canvas roof hides the daylight. But all I see is the hanging meat. Who knew so much was available, even here?

We allow ourselves to get swept along the narrow lanes, past the bakeries and fruit stalls. For a brief and blissful moment there is no war, no bombs or secrets. Mum was good at finding the right queue, without all the complaining and fussing. First we have to remove ourselves from the surge of shoppers. Somehow we manage it and, in front of a quiet stall, Timothy Squire and I take out our ID cards and ration books.

Timothy Squire has sixpence, and is gentleman enough to pay for us both. First we get tea (a penny), and then sausage sandwiches with brown sauce (threepence), for which we each surrender two meat points. We must find the perfect spot for such a meal.

Braving the crowd again, we make our slow way to sit before a large church. When pigeons immediately stagger towards us, Timothy waves them away. I eat as slowly as I can, fighting the urge to wolf it all down. The zing of the vinegar is delicious and warming. I try to think of Flo and her cherries. Timothy Squire smiles between mouthfuls.

When I thank him for his kindness he just brushes it off.

'Leslie is actually quite nice – what? Why that face?'

He is still grimacing. 'Nah. I don't get on much with that lot.'

What *lot*? The whole school? Without even thinking it my lips are forming the rhyme. 'Timothy Squire is a dirty old liar.'

He half smiles. '"Timothy Squire sings in the choir.

Timothy Squire died in the fire." Guess they think I'm always telling stories.'

'Oh,' I say when he finishes. 'I'm sorry.'

He shrugs. I look back down at my sandwich. *Died in a fire?* That's horrible.

'You could always come to the Bloody Tower.' I say, chewing too quickly. 'For breakfast. Everyone else does.'

'Breakfast?'

'What? You don't eat breakfast.'

'Yeah. At home.'

I shrug. 'I know. I just thought – if you didn't want to… you could always come to the Bloody Tower. Just ignore Oakes, that's what I do.'

Again he looks right at me. 'OK. Maybe, yeah.'

We are silent for a moment. Around us, traders shout their goods. I rack my thoughts, and then one of Uncle's particularly disgusting facts returns to me.

'A raven's beak is hard as steel… But it's not sharp at the end – not sharp enough to cut through the skin of a squirrel.' I watch Timothy Squire's eyebrows rise in inter-est. 'So how do you think they eat it? One morning Uncle walked on to the Green and found a perfectly complete, inside-out squirrel skin. A raven had torn the meat out through the squirrel's mouth.'

'Brilliant.'

If only I had asked Uncle for some money. The Chelsea buns smell *amazing*. I heard that full-time ARP wardens get £2 a week. (Does that annoying girl Violet really make

£2 a week? *And* she gets to wear that armband and tell everyone what to do?)

Timothy Squire would be fine at breakfast. He knows all the Warders already.

'So what do you think of Yeoman Oakes?' I hear myself asking.

'Oakes? He looks like a stick insect.'

'But do you... trust him?'

'What do you mean?'

'Do you think that maybe he could be a spy? A German spy?'

Timothy Squire nods as if considering it. 'Who wouldn't want a stick insect as a spy?'

'Forget it.'

'I don't like him either,' he says with a laugh. 'He'd be a terrible spy, though. Father says he's terrible at everything, even being a Warder. Everyone has spy fever – no one trusts anyone now.'

I offer a smile, feeling suddenly a little sad. I remind myself of Mum's insistence not to be narrow-minded. Uncle is a friend of Oakes, so clearly he can't be *that* terrible. And obviously Timothy Squire isn't threatened by him – so why should I be? I do *not* have spy fever. I could almost kick myself for being such a child. There are real enough worries without adding imaginary ones.

Too soon, we rise and begin the search for the butcher's stall. It is not too difficult to find, in the end, with its great queue snaking through the market. We join it, inching forward, Timothy Squire filling the time with various stories of his city adventures. When we reach the butcher, a surprisingly round man in a boater, he smiles down at us. He is still smiling as we leave.

'That was kicks,' Timothy Squire says, slipping the bag under his coat. 'Like the black market or something.'

As the crowds thin, the free, light air returns.

'Do you know what they sell in the black market?' I walk closer to him, my smile impossible to hide. 'Fingers. Human fingers! What anyone would want with a human finger, who can say, but it *is* wartime.'

He laughs, holds out his white hand. 'Not fingers, Magpie. Rings.'

'Rings,' I repeat slowly. Of course. How else to get them off? I feel a little silly, and Timothy Squire is still grinning as we once again enter the quiet streets. *He has bitten off nearly half his fingernails.* My mind is already turning, with nervous excitement, to the next task.

'The size of a palm,' I say, unwrapping the paper.

'Your palm, or mine?' he asks.

I pick up the meat, feel its slimy underside. What did Uncle say? *His* palm? I don't remember. Four ounces; how do you measure four ounces?

'Yours,' I decide. 'They have been good today. A treat.'

I am surprised by how difficult this suddenly is. *I can scale the Tower walls but can't prepare the meat for some birds?* I frown in concentration and Timothy Squire is grinning. With a sudden smile of my own, as though it only just occurred to me, I hold out the knife.

'Do you want to try?'

He is nodding and reaching in the same motion, and I feel my breath return. Of course I *could* have done it – I've watched Uncle do it a dozen times. Timothy Squire, though, looks to be doing a fair enough job.

'Now there's four ravens, remember – Cora, Edgar, Merlin, and Grip – so we'll need another pile here. They're used to traitors' corpses, remember? A pile here too. Good. Now let's go and round them up.'

I walk ahead, trying to keep a neutral face.

Off duty now, many of the Warders will have donned their city clothes and retired to the Tiger pub outside the West Gate. Some will be in the tavern just inside the Tower walls, playing darts or poring over *The Times* atlas, predicting and arguing. Uncle says there are no staff there; you simply sign your name and pour a beer. But I have wandered in and a Wife always seems to be at the bar, pulling pints and keeping a watchful eye on everything.

There is Nell again, walking with her swing, heels clicking, making her own way to the pub. (She is a *fire-watcher*, Leslie told me. The thought doesn't fill me with confidence.)

The wind screams around the stone. I walk faster for

warmth but I'm not really bothered. I'm feeding the
ravens with Timothy Squire. Most of the birds are there,
on the Green, watching me sail towards them.

'Once they're out, they're out,' I say.

Briefly attempting to whistle them over, I only succeed
in making a *shushing* noise. *I could do it yesterday.*
Timothy Squire turns to me and I quickly look away.

'They will come.'

Luckily, they do. The shiny black heads, marching at
my feet. As the sun drops straight down on the White
Tower we gather in the heavy shadows.

I lay down the food, trying not to think of the 'inside–
outside' squirrel story. *I have done this fifty times.*

Some minor squabbling ensues, with both Merlin and
Cora proving equally determined, while Grip eats alone,
black eyes gleaming. Merlin, with a low grunt, finally sur-
renders the extra portion to a gleeful Cora. Edgar gazes
around for more.

After a quick glance at me, Timothy Squire offers the
remaining biscuits. With a snap of the beak, the food is
taken. Timothy Squire lets out a delighted laugh, and
offers another round. The tilted glances cease, the birds
gather round the scraps. They seem to approve.

Standing with him amid the croaking birds, I feel a
certain *lightness*.

Once they have finished eating, it is time to put them
to bed. Merlin and Cora are already inside their cage,
and Edgar only needs some gentle encouragement. Grip,

though, is not in his usual area.

Looking round, I see him, walking heavily towards the Green. I wait a moment, watching, before I go to fetch him. Where is he going? I turn to Timothy Squire, still smiling, and twist back.

Grip, taking slow steps in the dusk, merges with the coming night.

The next morning I watch Oakes heading across the Green.

I almost laugh to think about it – that Oakes could be a spy. That a Nazi – in disguise or not – could march right up to the Tower of London to talk to him. The mystery of MacDonald's death is still unsolved, though.

My feet stumble. It is impossible. But I can tell, from across the Green, that it is true. There is a figure on the other side of the portcullis. A man. *The same man.* And Oakes is headed to meet him.

Dully, my eyes follow Oakes's blue uniform. I take a deep, shaky breath. I must get closer. I rush forward, cursing the echo of my shoes on the stone. A raven jeers; I ignore the sound.

I scurry to the side, out of sight, climb up the cut stairs of St Thomas's Tower, and push my way inside. In the sudden darkness I move across the creaking wooden floor. I must get *down* there. With lurching steps, I take the first stairs I find.

The narrow room is made smaller by all the ropes and pulleys leading below. I peer down – I can see nothing, but surely I will be able to hear them speak. I stand as close as I dare to the straining rope. The cruel black spikes shine in the darkness.

Even with my heart knocking furiously in my chest I can make out words. And a strange accent.

'I got a letter—'

'So did I,' comes Oakes's voice.

I inch closer, catching nothing else over the jeering raven. In my mind I throw a rock at him. *Not now.* Leaning forward, I place both hands against the cold metal. I can hear them again, clearly – their voices are raised.

'I'm beginning to think you don't have any cousins in Yorkshire.'

I bow my head. How can they sound so angry about something so boring? *Cousins in Yorkshire?* Why have a secret meeting at Traitors' Gate at low tide to talk about Yorkshire?

'Then again, you've never been known for your honesty, have you, Gregory?'

'Run back to Germany. If they see you here, you'll be shot.'

Again the raven's laughing croak. How is he so loud? It's as if he's in here with me.

The croaking goes on, the noise filling my ears. I abandon my position, hurry back down the stairs. There is no sound from the other side of the door, so I inch it open.

I pull it closed as Oakes sweeps past. He was moving quickly, *urgently*, away from the gateway. But I still saw it; his face red, and not just with anger. With fear.

My face must look the same. I was right all along. There is no doubt.

Oakes's secret friend is a German. Oakes is a spy.

I am frozen, unsure whether to go to Uncle straightaway. They are great friends. He will tell me I am being foolish, that my imagination is running away from me.

The man definitely had a German accent. And Oakes told him to go back to Germany. *If the others see you...* He is clearly hiding him, meeting him in secret. Why? Why else, but some kind of plan to aid Germany? Should I go to Sir Claud? Or maybe tell Yeoman Sparks? Surely I must go to Uncle first.

And if I do – will Oakes kill another bird? Cut off Grip's head?

I don't know. What I do know is that even if I tell him Uncle will not hear it. Even the best people refuse to hear what they don't want to.

He won't believe the truth.

Monday, 21 October 1940

I sit on my bench, the ravens scolding loudly, frantic for dinner. My mind races over what to tell Uncle.

Shocking me out of my daze, Malcolm, Yeoman Brodie's son and my supposed best mate, slinks towards me. He lowers himself on to the bench. Of course he does not speak.

'Long day at school?' I ask.

He shrugs. 'I suppose so.'

A raven hops in the distance. I can feel him watching it with his eyes.

'You don't like them, huh?'

Malcolm shakes his head vigorously. 'No. They tear up the grass, kill all the flowers.'

I look out over the bare Green, the grass dead for the season.

'They rip the putty out of the windows too. It is freezing in my room. We fix it, and they just steal it again. I hope they eat it and get sick.'

It is the longest sentence I have ever heard him speak.

A heavy silence falls. I squirm on the bench. Somehow even his muttering is preferable to the silence. *Surely dinner is almost ready.* One thing I have learned about Malcolm is his love of diamonds. He thinks the ravens are boring but loves diamonds and jewels – almost as much as Timothy Squire loves bombs. The residents of the Tower are strange people indeed.

'I wish I knew more about, you know, the Crown jewels,' I say, my voice hopelessly flat. He doesn't seem to notice or care.

'Do you know about the curse of the Koh-i-noor diamond?' he asks excitedly. When he peers up at you, he looks almost like a goat.

'The what?' I answer, knowing full well from one of Brodie's breakfast stories the name of the great diamond put in a brooch for Queen Victoria and then set in the crown of Queen Elizabeth.

'Koh-i-noor – "the Mountain of Light". Diamonds from the stone can only be used in a crown worn by a woman...'

Malcolm has plenty of new information as well, and soon I learn that he regrets that the Crown jewels are not here, certain that no 'secret' location can be safer than the Tower. But they are here, if you ask Uncle. *The ravens are the Crown jewels.*

A figure walks close by – Nell, all bobbed head and lipstick – and I have never been happier to see another person. Silence or this talk of diamonds – I can't take either for another moment.

'Nell,' I call, too loudly. She likely doesn't even know my name.

She doesn't seem to know Malcolm's either, by the look she gives us – two strangers gawking at her from a bench. She is wearing a blouse and short jacket, and navy-blue slacks with broad bottoms. I suddenly feel quite lumpy in my school uniform, which after another week of rations is definitely too big for me.

Nell walks closer, takes a Player's from the packet, lights it. Is she working as a firewatcher right now? She doesn't even have binoculars.

I am saved from thinking of an appropriate question by a growing sound. A droning. The drone grows louder. Countless dark shapes, like travelling black birds, cover the sun.

A terrific echo across the sky.

7

Stunned by the noise – it makes my knees ache – I look up at the barracks clock. It is only 4.05 p.m. The siren wails. This is a raid.

The ravens are still out.

Nell is bolt upright, her narrow shoulders raised, peering into the distance just beyond the turrets. My eyes follow hers. Thirty or forty planes at a great height. Close.

'Hitler thinks he's going to get me.' Nell shakes her head contemptuously. She does not call out or raise the alarm. It is too late. Bombers streak out of the clouds. Loud even to numb ears.

A few peel off and unleash their bombs. I watch as they fall like hammers from the sky. I cannot move. Explosions echo across the river. More planes harden from the clouds. Immediately the docks are on fire, black and red, climbing higher than the cranes. Smoke comes, surging towards the Tower, flooding over the old walls like sudden mist.

A rush of wings overhead.

I try to count the crashes; too many. We must get to the

shelter. The White Tower shelter, deep underground. But no one moves. I stare up at the barrage balloon, looming in the wind.

The stone suddenly jumps. A blast fifty feet ahead.

Another erupts just behind us, sending up a fountain of rock. Suddenly unfrozen, people hurry across the battlements towards the shelter. A Wife curses, a boy yells, Warders call for order. The ocean's roar of bombs silences everything.

The Tower is being attacked. We are too late.

I think of Oakes and the carving in the Salt Tower.

A map of the night sky.

With a series of shuddering bursts, shrapnel tears through the Inner Ward. The noise takes me to my knees. With terrible clearness I see a Scots Guard sink to the stone. I drag my gaze from the charred hair, the expressionless face, the sickening leak of blood.

More planes become visible through the distant clouds, a dozen at least, moving in formation. Everything becomes thunder. I kneel on the shaking stone, numb with terror.

The ravens.

Another, closer bang, and all the windows on the Martin Tower shatter, hurling glass towards us. Before my eyes snap shut, the explosion burns into my mind. Weightless, my body pushes forward, over the wet stone. I lie on my stomach, my knees torn, my elbows shredded. A screaming voice, now quiet and distant, finds me: 'To the shelter!'

Without the Tower ravens, the kingdom will fall.

My hands reach out, gripping rock. I blink my eyes open. People run around me, shrieking silently. Another explosion and a Wife in a shawl is thrown six feet in the air, landing in a white heap.

I try to stand only the blast pulls me to the stone – but at the same time *pushes* me, trying to force me apart. One of my shoes is gone, the wind hot on my sock foot. When I can I look up, to see a rolling bank of smoke over Salt Tower, twice as tall as the barrage balloon. The Main Guard burns. The stone, the cold bones of the Tower, are on fire.

I will die here. Burnt in some ancient fortress, away from Maida Vale and the canals, away from Flo, surrounded by the ghosts and ravens and lies. *Oh, Mum.*

For an eternity I am lost; eventually I come to my knees. I will not die here. I find my feet, swaying in the hot, scorched air. More bombers snarl in low over the turrets.

A blue hat vanishes in the flames and smoke, reappearing across the Inner Ward. My eyes cling to it. Lurching forward, I dodge several flaming craters. I can still see him, the Warder, running towards the shelter in the Casemates in the walls. Through the billowing smoke and burning stone, I follow.

I close my eyes against the heat, trapping the last sight in my mind. Smoke pouring from Salt Tower.

The daylight raid becomes a night raid. For hours the bombs fall.

We sit, some on chairs and the wood bench, some on the floor, filling the small room. Twenty-five people, doubled by the heavy shadows from the hurricane lamp. Uncle is here. *But where is Timothy Squire?*

No one goes to the electric kettle, and the newspapers lie unread. No one brings out the playing cards or takes aim at Hitler's pocked face on the dartboard. No one moves.

Dust slows my breathing and there is a crunching ache in my head. I think of the flames roaring outside, engulfing the Salt Tower.

Malcolm looks up at me. His voice is calm. 'I wonder how many of us will be alive in the morning?'

I say nothing. All I can think of is the Scots Guard, dying outside; the Wife, likely dying too. Others – how many others?

Uncle squeezes my hand. I am glad he is here. I must tell him I didn't have time to put the ravens in their cages. *Should I have brought them in here?*

A long ago image flashes in my mind, of the old man with the budgie at the school shelter, and deep, wild laughter threatens me. Instead I cough, hiding my face in my sleeve.

Malcolm speaks again, his voice eerily calm. 'Is it the invasion?'

We all pretend not to hear.

Clearly I can picture the NAAFI girls, laughing and

serving coffee at the canteen. What will happen to them? And Timothy Squire. Where is he? In the White Tower shelter, of course. Even he is not so foolish as to go hunting for bombs during a raid. *Timothy Squire died in the fire.* Who would lie about that?

And if this is finally the poison bomb raid? Will we be safe in here? My gas mask is under my bed with a cowering mouse. The ravens too must be terrified. No, I must think of something else. I look around. Uncle sits with Mr Brodie. Miss Breedon is here too, much older now and not nearly as pretty. No one else seems to have their masks either.

The Salt Tower was hit. A direct hit.

Hew Draper was not the sorcerer. It is Oakes. He has arranged all of this – Oakes and the German.

'There will be a second wave,' Brodie is saying. 'First they drop hundreds of the small bombs and wait for the emergency crews to come and put out the fires. Then the second wave attacks, this time delivering high explosives.'

No, those were not small bombs. I can still hear the thrashing outside. Some giant blind elephant, trampling us.

Mr Brodie leans in to me, smiles.

'You know, my dear, there are more than forty million people in Great Britain. Forty million, think of it. Even if the Jerries were better shots than they are, what are the chances of any one of us getting hit? Very small, indeed.'

I cannot look up, I cannot face him. The wild, gusting laughter is still inside me.

'It's not fear, you know,' Mr Brodie goes on. 'That feeling – that shaky, sick feeling. It's not fear. It happens to everyone during a raid.'

I can't hear any more consoling words about people being 'nervy'. I look down, my reactions still slow and dazed, and notice that the sock on my foot is striped red. Rolling down the thin wool, I find small spears of glass and much blood. Uncle takes down the first-aid box, wraps a bandage numerous times all round my foot. He dabs my elbows and knees with a towel; the cuts are minor.

'That better, dear?' he asks in a loud, slow voice and I nod. My ears buzz and ring. Uncle turns to the others, asking if everyone is all right.

Miss Breedon seems not to have heard him – or anything. She just stares at the floor, the dreadful sounds trembling around her.

Another night in the shelter. Like a new moon the bombs have returned. How can we ever believe they will stop?

I wake some hours later, aware of movement. It is Mr Brodie, stalking across the room, the heels of his heavy feet stomping in the silence. I think of Mum, pacing the kitchen, listening to the wireless. She always did that, from the day the war started. She was afraid, I know.

Yeoman Brodie sees me, slows to a stop, gives an apologetic smile. But it is Uncle who speaks.

'We are safe here, Anna,' he says.

The raid continues, now too loud for us to speak. Curdled and burnt, yet somehow still sweet, come the smells of the burning NAAFI canteen. *The tea.* As the night wears on the scent shifts from food, so carefully rationed, to the tobacco stores. And then things harder to burn – tables, beams, walls – mixed with the sudden and strong reek of urine.

Why are there no chamber pots in here? I remember once, we spent the *whole* night in the (already rusting) Anderson shelter, and Mum refused to take me inside to use the loo. Then at least it was summer. No, it couldn't have been; it felt like it, though, with warm night air and crickets in the hedge. Not like this, frozen and starved and smelling burning food all around us.

The bombs still fall, so close. I won't die here. With dust in my lungs and my ears whistling and my stomach empty. Without knowing what really happened to Mum, without finding out the truth.

And then it comes, simple as a great knock. I close my eyes, let my breath go.

Got you.

It is not a bomb, though. It is a knock, a knock on the shelter door.

Faces look round in confusion. Who could be out there in this? The German wouldn't bother to knock. A stone, loosened by a falling bomb, crashing against the shelter? *The invasion*?

Uncle steps forward. He opens the door. Someone *has* been outside, knocking on the shelter door, and now he stumbles inside. It is not a German soldier.

'Timothy Squire,' comes Uncle's startled voice. 'But... my God... I thought you were in the shelter with your father.'

He is breathing hard. 'I was.'

My gaze must give something away, as everyone is now looking at me, including Timothy Squire.

'Magpie.'

He moves towards the back of the room, sits across from me. Timothy Squire's question is as foolish as his grinning face.

'Well, now. Did you see *those* fireworks?'

Nobody yells, or warns him of his stupidity, or promises punishment. Not now. The only question I hear is one asked by Malcolm many hours ago. *How many of us will be alive in the morning?*

I know too that this is why Timothy Squire is here. I feel something, a shuffling. I pull my hand free of the blanket, and he grips it tightly. You could see my smile in the dark. If this is the invasion, we are ready.

Eventually, the raid is over, and time moves forward again. The All Clear, high and piercing, releases its hold.

We are alive, all of us. Uncle stands and pushes open the heavy door.

'Mind how you go, love,' he says, peering into the night. 'There's glass everywhere.'

'You have to be so careful,' someone says. 'If a gas mains is busted somewhere, a great explosion will not be far behind.' I glance behind me. I didn't see Miss Breedon leave, but she must have.

A haze of tobacco clouds and sailing debris dulls the flag atop the White Tower. Salt Tower is charred yet standing. Warders move among the splintered wood and clumps of stone, their uniforms grimy and grey. And above, somehow, a quiet sky littered with stars.

The thick dust makes me dizzy, and the whistle in my ears seems to grow and strengthen. My mind focuses on one thought. Maybe the ravens *did* know. The human spotters didn't see them coming. That is not possible, though, surely. 'Ravens are attuned to the sky,' Uncle said. It is another voice that pulls me back into the present.

'That was kicks.'

I look back towards the flag. Smoke curls up from the Green, black smoke. Something, deep down, tells me the truth.

I have failed them.

Without the ravens, the kingdom will fall.

Tuesday, 22 October 1940

A Scots Guard and a Wife were killed in the bombing. *I saw them both.*

I could not have helped them.

The birds, though, I could have helped. Edgar and Merlin – both dead. Shrapnel, Uncle said. I did not see the bodies. If I had just taken a moment to lure them inside, next to the shelter of the White Tower... would they have survived? It is a dreadful thought so I do not think it. Still it runs through my head.

Always there have been six ravens at the Tower.

Cora hops towards me, tilting an inquisitive head. Whether she can smell it or just sense it, I don't know. With a smile I pull out the twopenny chocolate from my pocket, breaking off a piece for each of us. She takes it, almost lightly, from my fingers.

The rest, though, is mine. She can have the wrapper. Days of burying and digging there. *It is only us now, Cora. You, me and Grip. Everyone else has left us.*

I sit heavily on the bench. The air is thick with drifting soot.

Many were injured, some quite badly. Dark smoke still clings to the ramparts. My head throbs and I fear that I will go deaf. But I am alive. For today, I am alive. I say a few silent words for the lost Scots Guard and Wife, and for the lost birds.

Goodbye, Edgar and Merlin.

Nothing feels warm enough. The sun itself is cold. And the ravens are dying – there is not enough food. Both have grown smaller; especially Cora, always the smallest. We are all starving.

Settled dust glows a faint red. The hammers are loud – fixing windows, rebuilding walls. Why, if Hitler is beginning his invasion?

'As long as they're bombing, we know they're not coming to invade. When they stop coming from the sky, I'll start looking to the sea,' said Mr Brodie at breakfast.

In the Great War, we learned at school, the French drove out the Germans. This time, it took Hitler less than a month to reach Paris. People weren't ordered to evacuate, yet the entire city fled, pouring from their homes in motor cars, on bicycles, on foot, blocking the roads *our* troops were trying to use to reach the city and defend it. Hitler walked into an empty city.

Where will they land? They must cross the sea, of course. Many people say the Germans will come from Ireland. And then?

To watch the snaking river is to constantly see their arrival, a sudden forming of soldiers from the mist. I see them now. They will come up the Thames, and we will not be ready. Everyone will flock to the bank to fight, old Mr Fraser and the rest of the Home Guard.

And what will we do? Uncle, Timothy Squire, two croaking ravens, and me?

Friday, 25 October 1940

'I think today is the day.'

While the voice belongs to Timothy Squire, the costume surely belongs to his father. Or grandfather. Today, instead of the checked cap, Timothy Squire sports an old golf cap. I am still used to the boy in the school uniform. His coat is the same, though, heavy and oversized.

He is standing in front of the thick walls of Wakefield Tower. His face too looks older – more serious. *What does he have planned?* The afternoon is calm and peaceful, and after the birds were fed, a sudden bright sun arrived. The ring in my ears has finally dulled away. Fresh air I would enjoy very much.

'Today is the day,' he repeats. 'For a Roman holiday. You know. Go and look at the ruins.'

Again I feel the warmth of escaping the Tower. And there are plenty of ruins to see. People, too poor and thin, wandering around. More than I have ever seen, even in the docks. Timothy Squire does not try to hold my hand. It would not be right, I realize, amid all these horrors. Or has something else changed? I wonder – I have been wondering for days – what Timothy Squire's father said to him. Maybe he took away his comics. I'm sure they had a dreadful row.

What would Mum have said to me? I would be in trouble *forever*. When I got in trouble for laughing at Piper Jones in first form, she was quite shocking about it. What would Father have said to me?

The thought dies instantly. I know nothing about Father. Mum only talked about how he played the violin and he was a sailor. And he drowned in the North Sea.

Timothy Squire has the same carefree lope as always. Something, though, is different. Maybe Sir Claud spoke to him. Leaving the shelter is never allowed.

The Tower has changed. Everyone is on edge.

The NAAFI girls are fine, though the fire destroyed the canteen. Yeoman Cecil has been grumbling that 500,000 cigarettes were lost in the flames. The moat too had been bombed, clearing the Women's Royal Airforce detachment from their huts. The barrage balloon went with them.

I think back to how I felt the night before the raid. A sense of excitement, of the possibility that things could get better. And when Timothy Squire appeared like a reckless fool at the shelter, even then, though it seemed certain that a bomb would get us... there was something. A hope.

Now I feel rattled like everyone around me. It's easy to tell yourself things will work out OK, quite another thing to believe it.

Hope is a good breakfast but a bad supper.

Before I have a chance to try asking him, Timothy Squire stops in front of a destroyed building. A whole house, I realize, fallen into the basement. He prowls amid the ruin, lifting up pieces for inspection.

We move on down a twisting road that Flo would have called a 'slummy street'. Another row of flats, recently hit. The firemen must have only just left. Sun shines in the gap where something – a church? – once stood. Everywhere else, the air is heavy, almost black.

'Timothy Squire. I have to talk to you – about Oakes.'

'The spy?' he says, dripping sarcasm.

'He met with a German.' I plough ahead. 'I heard them. Outside Traitors' Gate.'

'Traitors' Gate?' I can hear the smile. 'Well? What did he say?'

'He said – Oakes said he'd shoot him if he didn't go back to Germany.'

'Doubt it.'

'What?'

'Dad says Oakes is practically a pacifist. Anyway what's the problem? If some German has parachuted into the city, Oakes is right to chase him off. 'Course, he should've shot him dead there and then, but it's Oakes after all…'

As he wanders off I stare around, mesmerized. It is strange to find myself smiling. Am I hoping this same destruction has visited Germany?

Blinking in the sun, I realize that Timothy Squire has got himself on top of a pile of rubble. He looks strong, important, up there. It takes me a moment to realize that he is peering into the window of the ruined flat opposite. He turns, catches my glance.

'Come on,' he says.

'Where?' To see more broken bricks and clouds of dust?

Timothy Squire walks round to the front of the house, pushing cautiously against the door.

'Timothy Squire,' I call out. He has already gone inside.

I twist, looking wildly around. If one of the firemen returns, or the ARP Warden passes by, they will think...

Timothy Squire's round face appears in the glassless window.

'Come on.'

I step inside. The ceiling light still shines, revealing Timothy Squire in the corner.

'Too late,' he mutters.

Too late? The fires have only been out a few hours. Too late for what?

He is at something – the gas meters – but they are broken. He moves quickly away, pushing the rubble aside with his foot. The light, though dim, seems far too strong now.

'What are you doing?'

'I read something... Ah,' he says, unearthing a faintly recognizable object. A purse, which he turns open. Empty.

155

'Timothy Squire,' I say in a low voice, 'let's get out. Now.'

He continues to search the room. I stay near the door, casting glances behind me.

'We have to leave,' I say, suddenly very scared. 'We could go to prison.'

'What? For scrounging?'

'Bloody hell.'

My heart drums in my ears. If someone comes I won't be able to hear.

We are looters.

He smiles, still looking. 'Much good it's going to do this lot.'

My breath is short, too short.

'Looting...'

'Nothing here to loot, I'd say.'

Despite his words, he keeps searching. A noise comes from behind me – I'm sure of it – but no one is there. Yet. Why is he doing this? Is he *determined* to go to gaol?

'Well, well.' An exaggerated intake of breath. 'Someone left in a hurry. Dropped this.'

He holds up, too impossible and bizarre to imagine in the setting, an orange. Gloriously bright and round, a tiny sun.

'Who else is going to claim it? Rats? We have to look after ourselves.'

He almost sneers the words. *Maybe he is right.* With Warders helping spies and Uncle refusing to listen – if we don't look after ourselves, who will?

His tone changes as he sees my face. 'We're just like the birds. Storing up for the winter.'

I can say nothing. Would Mabel steal from the dead? The answer is more definite than I'd hoped.

'Come on,' he says, pocketing the orange. The room is suddenly darker, colder. 'I bet there's more back here.'

There is more. I follow, slowly at first, then quickly. A lipstick. A lighter. Four stamps at twopence-halfpenny. All covered in dust, all slipped into the pockets of Timothy Squire's oversized coat.

We sneak out silently. The sun glares. I have no time to think; all I know is that we have to get back to the Tower.

'All right, you lot.'

I freeze at the voice. I expect Timothy Squire, who is several steps ahead of me, to dash off down the alley. Instead he turns and smiles up at the ARP Warden.

'Good evening, sir.'

'Aye, is it? And what are you up to here, lad?'

'Nothing, sir.'

He smiles threateningly. 'I'll be the judge of that, won't I? What are you two children crawling among the rubble for? You lining your pockets?'

Despite how pale Timothy Squire looks, his smile never

leaves. 'No, sir. No use for rocks, not unless Hitler's planes start flying lower.'

'Boy, you're fooling nobody. You are in real trouble, you understand me?'

He seems to. His face passes to a further, improbable shade of white. His words seem to have drained away with his blood.

I smile, stepping forward. 'I'm so sorry, sir. Truly, it is all my fault. I just asked if he would show me around. I'm not from here, you see...'

Of course he does see, from the moment I open my mouth, a West London girl in the East End, and his anger turns to scorn.

'Christ. A good evening to be out sightseeing, is it?'

'No, no, sir. Just headed home for dinner now. I am sorry to have caused any problem.'

'I'm so tired of you gawkers, having fun from someone else's misery. This isn't a show, you understand.'

He points to Timothy Squire.

'Don't you go helping this lot get their entertainment. You'd be right to be ashamed, the two of you. Now find your legs, on you go. Move.'

We turn and leave without another word. My face burns.

IV

THE FIRE AND THE MOON

If this invasion is going to be tried at all, it does not seem that it can be long delayed.

It ranks with the days when the Spanish Armada was approaching the Channel, and Drake was finishing his game of bowls; or when Nelson stood between us and Napoleon's Grand Army at Boulogne.

We have all read about this in the history books; but what is happening now is on a far greater scale and of far more consequence to the life and future of the world and its civilization than these brave old days of the past.

– Churchill, broadcast to London, 11 September 1940

8

Monday, 28 October 1940

Across the table, the *Daily Mirror* headline screams out: *Hang a Looter and Stop this Filthy Crime*. A quick glance says it all. Those found guilty of looting from homes damaged or vacated for reasons of enemy attack will suffer prison or death. At least I see no articles about the ravens – how they are dying. How the kingdom is falling.

I shift uncomfortably on the bench, looking around the Stone Kitchen, away from the newspapers. Again Uncle is not at breakfast. I am beginning to worry that he might become an invalid like Mum's friend, Ester. The Warders chat, the plates have been cleared, and I fear I will soon be left alone with Oakes.

It pains me to admit it; Timothy Squire is right. While Oakes may have met with a German, he also threatened to kill him. He can't be a traitor then, can he? And one can't be friends with a German. When it turned out that Mrs

Weber across the street had an Austrian husband, he was sent to the Isle of Man, and she moved out to live in Surrey. It is not possible that Oakes helped coordinate the raid. *It was pure chance that Salt Tower was hit.* Oakes has even been gracious enough not to mention my accusation about MacDonald.

As the talk and laughter dies down, the other two Warders stand and leave. We are alone. Perhaps Uncle will arrive to remove the newspapers with a great flourish, insisting that I have no need to read them. *To hide them from me.*

Instead Oakes takes out a handkerchief, blowing his nose for a loud and impossible length of time. No one arrives. He puts his elbows on the table, leans slightly forward.

'Well, Anna...'

I collect the remaining cutlery as Oakes takes up the brush and Vim. Whenever Flo's father would say one of those things I didn't quite understand, he would smile and add, 'Something to think about while you help your mum with the dishes.' Now, though, no thoughts come. The scrape of the plate fills the world.

The whole walk back with Timothy Squire, I didn't say a word. Now, of course, I am bursting with all the things I should have said. That he is an idiot. That what he did was disgusting. The question rises up, refuses to go away. *He paid for the sausage.* I think too of his strange caps and mismatched blazers. How long has he been doing this? What do his parents think?

Silence reigns as Oakes deposits plates into the luke-warm water.

He pauses and holds up a dirty knife, staring as if seeing one for the first time.

'Imagine,' he says softly, 'doing that – with this.'

The cup slips clattering from my hands. *MacDonald.*

'What do you mean?'

He smiles, dropping the knife into the rapidly disap-pearing foam. 'The carving, Anna. Have you forgotten about Hew Draper so soon?'

I fight the urge to step back. *Why is he talking about the carving?* Or is he really talking about MacDonald? Even a sneak like Oakes isn't likely to brag to a thirteen-year-old girl about how he murdered a raven. *I am not scared of him.*

'Do you know the legend of King Arthur, Yeoman Oakes?'

'Not all of them, I'm sure,' he smiles, trying to hide his disapproval of my tone.

'That he is destined to return, some day, as a raven. So you must never harm one.'

He sighs, a deep, heavy sigh. 'Your uncle is the first "Ravenmaster", did you know that? Before that, his title was plain old "Quartermaster". He loves those birds.'

Of course. Oakes would never do anything to hurt Uncle. After scrubbing the final few knives and spoons, I wait to release the plug. Always there is an errant fork somewhere.

Once, when I was ten, and Mum had annoyed me by not letting me go to see *The Adventures of Robin Hood*, I thought about her dying. Except in my mind I moved in with Flo, and she became my sister, and her parents were happy and laughing as they watched us play. Flo's mum was never mean or yelled even one time.

I don't know what's come over me; suddenly I feel very brazen.

'Yeoman Oakes, sir?'

'Yes, Anna?' He arranges the pots on the tea towel, leaving them to dry in the chill air.

'Do you... do you know why he fought with my mother?'

The expression that passes over Oakes's face changes it completely. 'I don't, Anna. You really should not be asking such questions. The business of adults—'

'I know. I am sorry, sir. I am. But Uncle tells me nothing.'

'Anna... I never met your parents. Your mother was a wonderful woman, an extraordinarily brave woman, who championed unpopular causes and always fought for the truth. Do not think poorly of her.'

Oakes mutters some words about the long day ahead and quickly leaves me standing alone in the kitchen. I release the plug and with a low gurgle the dirty water drains away.

I have, without meaning to, come to the roost. Cora perches atop the inner wall. The sharp wind that tears the clouds above only ruffles her wings. She stays firm, claws curled, head cocked.

It is not time for her feeding. More than bombs and smells and traitors, it is the lack of food that has made her life different. *Does she understand why? How the world is different?*

The sun shines, yet it no longer bounces off her, no longer reveals the deep blue polish that is her true colour. Other birds look fragile; not ravens. Ravens are hard, sturdy – survivors.

I stand there, staring at the plane trees, slowly blinking away hot tears.

It's a bloody bird! Mum was killed, and Father drowned before I was old enough to even remember his face, and I am crying over a bloody dying bird.

No. Cora is not dying.

Not while I am looking after her.

School is hellish. My workbook is almost full and I've taken to borrowing paper from Leslie. This at least gives her a chance to tell me more stories. Even though raids have become a dreadful bore, Leslie still makes a fuss over every one.

'Another Tube station was hit,' she says, handing me three sheets. 'Sloane Square. Got people just as they stepped off the train.'

'Horrible.'

She leans in. 'Everyone died. Thrown all over, some on the live wires. And what's worse, the explosion tore off all their clothes, so there's just naked bodies hanging from the girders.'

'Hanging?'

'If you're lucky. Most of what they found were just bits. A foot on the tracks, an arm on the platform. They sweep them all up in a dustpan.'

Leslie has many stories like this. Two left feet found in a gutter, a torso on a rooftop – and, everyone's greatest fear, people buried alive. She is not trying to scare me, not really, as much as she is showing that *she* is not afraid. But as she talks her face is more drawn than usual.

Even as I listen, my eyes wander to Timothy Squire who, as always, stares straight ahead. *What is he thinking? What is he planning?*

At least I know why he didn't want to take me to the docks on my birthday. He'd just been down there, looting. *That* is why he missed Churchill's visit. Those things, glittering in his closet – watches and bracelets, not bombs. He is not a bomb expert. He is a thief. He *is* a rotten liar.

Who cares? Things outside are worse. Other stories and rumours besides Leslie's have reached us. Of boroughs where water is unsafe to drink, where it must be boiled only there's no gas to do so. Oakes goes on about it over breakfast. Still, it is exhausting to worry about the other boroughs, the other cities.

During a break in Leslie's stories, I whisper, 'Will they invade? Truly?'

'Doubt it, myself,' she answers slowly. 'They haven't yet, and my father says it makes less and less sense. Longer nights and high tides, sea mists and fog.' She shrugs. 'But it's Hitler, so.'

How long can we wait, bombed every night, for the Germans to invade? A headache is coming.

Germans can't invade across the channel, Uncle said. The North Sea is our greatest ally. The Old Man has been a friend to British sailors for hundreds of years, now it protects us all. *That is how much he cared for Father. He doesn't even remember that the North Sea killed him.*

I am tired. Tired of Timothy Squire lying to me, of everyone lying to me. Tired of being here, waiting for the next dreadful attack.

Miss Breedon calls us back to attention, but no Latin exercise can distract me.

Timothy Squire will ask again. He will want you to come.

What can I say?

I open Cora's cage. I know right away, of course. No movement, no croaking of her thick noise.

I peer inside just long enough to see her, sideways in the straw nest, rigid and unmoving. I step away, heading towards the Green, the scaffold, the walls, my breath catching in my chest.

I must tell Uncle. I should have told him before, when there was still time.

It was not time she needed. It was food.

Before I was brought to the Tower, two other ravens had died in a bombing raid ('the spares'). Cora, who used to sleep under the boilerhouse with one of the spares, was brought to the cage so that they could all be together. Cora was always the smallest, the most shy. Now she too is gone.

Kraa.

I back away from Grip's sharp challenge. Does he, too, blame me? Grip and I stand, facing off, in the slashing wind.

With a final cry, he stomps away, towards the dark teeth of the battlements.

I am alone on the Green.

Thursday, 31 October 1940

'Where are we going?'

Timothy Squire's voice floats back to me on the cold air. 'Not far.'

We've already gone far. So far, in fact, that I can no longer see the Tower on the horizon. Blitz streets all look the same. Sandbags and barbed wire with gardens dug up for allotments. I was never quite sure, when Flo and I ventured out along the canals, where exactly to turn and when. Without her it was often a sight – a tree here, a yellow boat there – that helped guide me back home.

Why I am here at all is the real question. Timothy Squire lied to me. He doesn't really care about bombs or comics – only robbing people. He never talks to me at school, or in front of anyone else. And all these friends he's always telling stories about? I've never seen a single one.

So why am I here?

Bridges slide past and we keep walking, tracing the loop of the river. Timothy Squire does not search the landscape for clues. He stalks the streets without doubt, without wrong turns or confusion. I am silent, tracking the route in my mind. Few people wander the streets. The pubs too seem empty.

Is that Pimlico Station? We are close to Victoria Station then. I can imagine it, crowded with people carrying suitcases, trying to get the hell out. People are going to Hampstead, Leslie says, just to live in the fields. It is fearsomely cold, as the wind musters itself for another winter. If it gets as bad as last year, I don't know how you could survive in a field.

'Come on,' he says. 'This way.'

One thing is certain; these houses are not bombed out.

This does nothing to calm me, though, as Timothy Squire's intention is clear. I never told him how much I hate this. 'This is different,' he will claim. The tall, stately house fronts, the window sills full of pots, the flowers long dead, seem to prove it. This neighbourhood is untouched.

He is scared, that is all. He thinks the invasion is coming. That we need food, supplies – as much as we can get our hands on.

He might be right.

If I'd come with him more often, maybe I could have saved Cora.

No. I could not have fed Cora some old lady's necklace.

Timothy Squire looks to have found something to his liking. He strides up to a semi-detached house, presses his face up to the white shutters. Is it abandoned, though? With so much moving, so much coming and going, who knows if the people have really left? Why would you leave such a safe area?

'Dust covers,' he says triumphantly.

We sneak round the back. I do not want to watch to see what he does, but he calls me closer.

'Look. Getting through a locked door is nothing.'

He holds up a long rusty nail, slides it into the keyhole.

'Just sweep it around until you feel the catch, then twist – and push.'

The door creaks open. I stagger ahead, as if a spell is broken.

We will not be able to trick the wardens here.

We stand in a drawing room with a red and yellow rug, glass-fronted bookcases, and some type of Indian statue staring back at us. The room is cold. Like the Tower, in a way. Long abandoned, perhaps. Is this what a house feels like left empty and unused?

Timothy Squire knocks the money out of the gas meters. Long moments pass as he fusses with the coins.

'What if they come back?'

'"Come back"?' He laughs, high and humourless. 'Once the invasion starts, all this will belong to the Jerries. Better off with us than with Hitler.'

'If you're so sure we're all going to die, why do you need other people's trinkets?'

He looks up at me, serious. 'I am not going to let us die.'

I frown, say nothing.

A radio, he claims, is what this is all about. *For our safety.* I wander round as he finds one, shoves it into his pack. *Why can't he just use the wireless at the Tower?* I see something in the wardrobe. A coat, maybe for a girl or a short woman. Warm, full-length and a nice lilac colour. Why wouldn't they take it with them? Do they really have no need for a beautiful warm coat in this freezing weather?

I look but I can't see Timothy Squire anywhere. The coat *is* too long, but it is not unwearable. Mum would love it. The softness of the sleeve.

On the walk back to the Tower, Timothy Squire keeps glancing at me.

'This stuff is better off with us, Magpie.'

I shake my head. He says 'us' even though I did not take the coat. I watch him through narrowed eyes. He strolls along, arms swinging, new treasures in his pockets.

He is afraid of the invasion. That is why is he acting like this.

We are all afraid. *We don't all rob people.*

'Timothy Squire,' I say, as we hurry through the cold, 'you must promise me. Promise you will never do that again.'

He makes a face. 'No. Why would I?'

'Because it's horrid. And wrong.'

'No, it's—'

'I mean it. Promise.'

'Who else is going—'

I look over at him, his large forehead red from the wind.

'Promise me. You won't.'

He makes another face, but it changes, softens.

'Fine. Right. I promise.'

9

Sunday, 3 November 1940

Red as a fox, her hair catches the lamplight. In the doorway, I watch her. I struggle yet cannot move. Just then she sees me. In the night, silently, Mum rises to hug me.

I lie exhausted in the black cold of my room.

I brace for other images but none come. Just the wind, ceaseless, moaning, slipping through the stone. It does not sleep either. I roll stiffly on to my side and then to my feet. The long winter night has ended. Wrenching aside the blackout curtain, I stare at the day. Sunday dawns grey and wet.

I look up at the heavy sky, frowning. How can there be that much dust – enough dust to block out the sun?

The silence of the Tower surrounds me. Wind on stone, shuffling echoes.

By nightfall the clouds have cleared. The black sky is empty. Searchlights stab and point in the darkness. No planes fly. No bombs fall.

Fifty-seven straight days. Every night, they have come.

Is it over? Have the Germans given up? Can people come up from the Underground, turn on their lights, go outside?

Or is Timothy Squire right? Is this the invasion?

When they stop coming from the sky, I'll start looking to the sea.

I push aside Brodie's words. I am happy, for a moment, to watch the small stars shining out. Tonight, for the first time in almost a week, I will shake out my hair and have a bath. Maybe I will wear it long, like Mum's, even though I don't have her lovely curls.

One thing I know for certain. Tonight, for the first time since I have lived at the Tower, I will go to sleep in my pyjamas.

The cold sun shines. The Warders, now all smiles and chuckling laughter, have gathered on the Green for a game of bowls. Grip and I watch them suspiciously.

Even Uncle is here, and though his throw is well short, he laughs as loud as the others. Oakes cheers him on with a grin I didn't know he possessed. The sky is quiet, a gentle blue.

It is nice to be away from Timothy Squire, to be free of the stiffness of spending time with him. Stealing and sneaking and hiding.

Even some of the Wives are here, though few are smiling.

The Wives should be happier – most husbands are away in the desert or God-knows-where. Their husbands are alive and nearby. Other wives have to wait for letters from abroad, living in fear that some horrid news will come. No, it is not so bad for the Wives. They just have to waste away in queues.

I must stop thinking poorly of the Wives. *I* don't want to spend all day in the queues, sorting out food coupons. Many of the Wives belong to the WVS, mobile squads of nurses, and committees that look after the refugees (French and Belgian, Leslie says). And many of the Yeoman Warders *are* in danger, leaving the Tower for second jobs as ARP wardens or firewatchers, members of rescue parties or volunteer firemen like Oakes.

Eventually, I am invited to try my hand – Yeoman Cecil is quite insistent – and I wander over and do my best. I send the ball as far as I can (much further than Uncle's), yet still shy of the mark. There are many smiles, though, and soon I feel myself smiling too.

Though I have always burned easily in the sun, I don't move into the shade until the game is over.

Dinners have become even worse. It seems raw carrots and potatoes are about the only things left. I don't even wait to get back to my room. I have half a twopenny chocolate bar hidden inside my coat. (From Uncle.) The Warders, arguing and clearing up, are paying no attention to me. Unwrapping the chocolate, I take a slow, deliberate bite; then chew as fast as I can.

Uncle, pottering around the room, stops me as I leave. A little guiltily, I keep my head down as he talks.

'I have something for you.'

He gives me a box. Inside, gleaming in the candlelight, is a knife. *A bare bodkin.* Delicately, he reaches for it, lifts it free. He turns it slowly over.

'The handle is of yew, the same wood as the longbows of the famous yeoman archers.' He presses the handle, gently, into my palm. 'Happy birthday.'

My expression says something that my mouth doesn't, because he carries on in a low tone.

'Just promise to keep it safe in its box.'

'I will, Uncle.'

I know why he is giving this to me. I remember the rest of Churchill's words. *A bare bodkin for every hand. If the*

Hun is to come, they will come. You can always take one with you.

Is this a fake peace? Is the invasion about to begin? When Flo and I were in Brighton, everyone still called it the 'phoney war' and the 'bore war'. We were rushed back to London when Hitler invaded Belgium.

I remember thinking the war was going to be fine. I remember, early in June, the photographs in all the papers of the massive numbers of Canadians and Australians arriving in Britain. We were going to win.

Looking down at the small knife in its box, my eyes dim with tears.

Thursday, 14 November 1940

After school, I sit with Timothy Squire up on the battlements. He rarely leaves the grounds lately, I've noticed. Certainly not with me. We haven't spoken a word to each other since I made him promise to stop looting. When he once came up and stood right in front of me, he saw the expression on my face and said nothing. Probably looking for someone to play Monopoly with.

Today, though, we are sitting together in full view of the Tower.

'It's not right,' he says.

'What?'

'Something is wrong. Can't you feel it?'

Yes. 'Uncle gave me a knife as a birthday gift.'

His eyebrows climb.

The winter has hardened and so has the mood. After the single night of peace the Germans have returned, but now the attacks seem minor, brief. When Leslie said last week was the quietest Guy Fawkes Night she'd ever heard, neither of us laughed. No one seems to laugh these days. Something *is* wrong.

In the distance, a figure leans against the wall. It is Nell, not doing her firewatcher duty. It is clear, even at this distance, that she is ashing her cigarette.

'You have to come and see.'

'See what?' I say, turning back to him. Some more shrapnel? A lady's pearls?

Together we slide from the wall and head towards the barracks.

Again there is no one home. He is rummaging around in the pile of comics. It is not a comic that emerges. I recognize the radio instantly. The Warders have stopped listening to the BBC – grown tired of the jolly stories from the shelters, according to Oakes. One more resounding tale of 'Blitz spirit' will be enough to send people rioting in the streets. Oakes is spreading defeatism, I suppose, in his delusional attempts to stop the war.

Uplifting tales of heroism are not what Timothy Squire wants me to hear.

A voice crackles from the speakers.

'Germany calling. Germany calling.'

I recognize the voice, which sounds more like 'Jairmany calling', and I immediately jump to my feet.

'We can't listen—'

'I told you, they don't tell us anything.' Timothy Squire's voice has that sneer in it.

'Well, I believe you. But I don't want to listen to this.'

Lord Haw-Haw (I've never heard his real name) does a daily broadcast from Radio Hamburg. We are told not to listen to Nazi propaganda, though some people seem to – I can sometimes hear his voice when I sneak past the barracks. Leslie laughs at him, how wrong and desperate he is. Others whisper about it, about how Lord Haw-Haw knows things that the BBC won't tell us.

'It's unpatriotic,' I say.

'Something is going to happen,' says Timothy Squire.

He is just scared, I tell myself. Still, it doesn't feel right to be listening to this. *Why, Timothy Squire, must you be so awful?*

Lord Haw-Haw's voice is nasal, like someone talking with a busted nose (definitely *not* the velvety voice of Bruce Belfrage on the BBC), but his threats are chilling.

'The Jews will get it tomorrow. The bombers will be over the Morris works in Oxford, and then on to Southampton.'

Bombs *are* falling all over Britain. London has had a

few nights of anxious peace, but larger raids have targeted other cities. Birmingham, Manchester, Coventry, Bristol, Sheffield – attacking coal miners, shipbuilders, and steel workers. The radio voice is gleeful.

'When Southampton is finished, Winchester will be next. But Hitler has something special for you tonight.'

Timothy Squire's eyes are on me. He looks, for the first time, openly frightened.

'Something is going to happen,' he says.

I don't know what to say. *Something* always happens. Why is this different? Unless… are they truly coming?

'What do you think?' I ask, trying to sound casual.

He shakes his head. 'I don't know. But something *different*.'

'It's Oakes,' I say suddenly.

Timothy Squire does not turn off the wireless.

'Oakes?'

'Yes. Meeting with that German—'

'Traitors' Gate?' Again the smirk in the words.

'Yes, at bloody Traitors' Gate! Listen, every time we're hit… there's a connection. I don't care about spy fever – Oakes is a spy, I'm sure of it.'

'So what do you want me to do?' he says meanly, making that sickening gesture across his throat.

MacDonald.

I am suddenly filled with a terrifying thought. *No. I am acting mad.* Timothy Squire steals from empty houses; he would *never* kill MacDonald.

180

The thought is not as convincing as I'd hoped.

In the silence, the nasal voice returns, sneering.

'Hitler has given you a day to bury your dead. Yesterday was only a sample.'

Where was yesterday's attack? Are bombers coming back to London? I leave Timothy Squire's flat without saying goodbye.

Back in my room, several hours later, I pull back the blackout curtain. The moon, huge and white, is rising. Too big, too fast. At any moment, the wail of the siren will be heard. Any second now, the Tower alarm will sound.

The night deepens. I check again, carefully, and see the moon shining cold and cruel. My eyes ache with the strain. And then, a sound. High, metallic, distant. Bombers. They are here.

But nothing comes. A far-off ship, perhaps. Or a distant plane, intent on some other mission? I stay at the window, unafraid of Violet or Uncle spotting me, my legs beginning to shake.

Searchlights, over and over, stab the sky. It is empty.

Friday, 15 November 1940

Nothing has happened.

A trick? Perhaps they will come tonight instead, wear us down with waiting and guessing. While at breakfast I learn the truth. They did come. Only not to London.

'Coventry,' Uncle says, his voice low, 'is destroyed.'

'Destroyed?'

'Gone. They came in waves. Ten hours. There is nothing left.'

The rest of breakfast is eaten in silence. This time Yeoman Cecil does not call it an 'incident'. Even Oakes fails to point out some flaw of Churchill's that is at the root of it all. At least until the plates are cleared away, when he seems to have come up with something.

'That'll be for Munich, which we bombed last week. Throw a punch, take a punch, throw a punch. Churchill and Hitler's great boxing match.'

No one bothers to respond. It must truly be awful. How many casualties? Hundreds? Thousands? I hear that horrible voice in my head. *Jairmany calling.*

Timothy Squire seems quite pleased when I see him on the Green. He goes on and on about how he suspected something, how no one is being honest. I am too hungry to tell him to shut up. Is he right, though? Are we being lied to? Are we all just waiting to die? Coventry is gone, and London might be next.

What is the point of just waiting – starving – for the Germans to come.

He looks across the bench at me.

'I am hungry,' I say.

'There is no food in the Tower.'

I say nothing, yet Timothy Squire sees something in my look. Without a word, he nods.

'Today after school,' he says, standing.

I watch him go before hurrying after him to class.

Timothy Squire and I shiver through a ruined flat. Nothing is inside, no clothing, no food – not a crumb. Only the wind at the cracked window. There is enough light to see clearly Timothy Squire's tired face. How long has he been doing this? How long has he been so horrible? *You are no better now.*

'Don't move.'

My entire body trembles.

'I see you. You're both dead.'

A woman appears, a broomstick in hand. The whole world shrinks.

'They told me to leave, that my house would be safe. That no one would try to rob me.'

She stumbles in, cuts off the doorway. Why? Why is she standing in the doorway? We are two robbers, killers as far as she knows. *Move.*

She doesn't. She is a rock, cutting off our escape.

No, she is inching closer, approaching us.

Timothy Squire is making a sign at me, but I'm not looking at him. I see now, on the table amid the dust, a coloured photograph in a silver frame. The woman, in the back, with her husband and two young children. The woman's hair is long, much longer than it is now, and though she is not smiling you can feel her happiness.

Timothy Squire whispers, a harsh sound – '*Magpie*' – and I finally turn.

The woman is close now, broomstick raised, threatening. And then it happens. In Timothy Squire's hands, shining in the light.

My knife.

The dusk light is impossibly bright. Timothy Squire is still pale, casting backwards glances as we run. After we are well free of the neighbourhood, I gesture for him to stop.

'You all right?' he pants.

I time it perfectly, and my fist connects, hard, with his stomach. He stumbles, falls to his knees on the wet pavement. Although his grip is strong I have taken him by surprise, and soon the knife is in my hands.

'Are you mad?' he cries out, a hand clutching his gut as he rises to his feet. 'You could've sliced your hand off—'

'I'll slice off yours if you ever steal from me again,' I gasp for air, putting the knife in my bag. 'Don't steal from people – from homes—'

'There's nobody in them!' he says, the pain clear in his face. 'Jesus.'

'That only makes it worse.'

We walk on. My face burns. *There was someone inside* that *house. Has he forgotten that already? Is he really* that *stupid? He threatened a woman with a knife in her own home so that we could run away.*

'It's horrible,' I say.

I sense his anger, but he says nothing.

'And you're horrible for doing it. How did you get my knife? Don't *ever* go into my room.'

I think of the diary under the bed. The things I've written, about Mum, about how scared I am – the things I've written about *him.*

'It was in case – in case something like *that* happened,' he is still holding his gut. 'You said your uncle got you one, so I – bloody hell, Anna. That hurt.'

'You *expected* to run into people?'

'So you want to just starve, waiting for the Germans to come—'

'You are a coward, Timothy Squire. You hide in your comic-book world and collect bombs and make up stories like it's all a game – and now that you can't hide any more, you go mad, and steal from people and threaten them with knives! You only care about yourself.'

Timothy Squire has a wild look in his eyes. 'What about you? You want to run away but you're too scared. You think Oakes is a spy and you do nothing because you're frightened. You don't care about anyone either.'

'You have your mum and dad, and all the stupid NAAFI girls. I have no one. Who should I care about? *You?*'

He looks at me, looks down. 'Stop whinging. You have your uncle, who cares about you enough to make up a whole legend just to keep you happy. All that stuff about the ravens just to make you think you're helping – that you *can* help. We all do what we have to.'

'Is that why you killed Raven MacDonald?'

'I didn't kill your stupid bird.'

'MacDonald was *so* much smarter than you. You are a dirty liar.'

We are not looking at each other now, but staring at the street ahead. All I can picture is MacDonald when I found him. His head cut off by a knife. Dumped in the ditch like rubbish. I say the next words, slowly, calmly.

'You should not have come to the shelter that night. I wish you never had.'

As we walk I feel his pace slowing, falling out of step. Looking forward, I keep walking, step after step, through the thickening snow.

Finally, reaching a corner where I can quickly glance back, I see that he is not there. Without thinking, I stop and turn, looking down the street, into the dusk.

He is gone.

10

Tuesday, 24 December 1940

'It's nothing, you know,' says Yeoman Cecil over breakfast. 'This rationing. You should have seen us in the Depression. Half starved, everyone was, in the Hungry Thirties. You practically needed to steal in order to survive. We all pinched a bit of food back then.'

Even though I feel that the words are meant for me, of course they are not. *No one would excuse Timothy Squire's looting.*

Despite his grumbling, Yeoman Cecil is in an excellent mood. He received a message that his son is safe in a PoW camp. 'The Christmas miracle,' he calls it.

We have just listened to the ration-book cooking tips that follow the 8 a.m. news. Today they gave Christmas recipes. Although no truce has been brokered – no football match on the Western Front, no laying down of arms – one seems to be implied. Even Nell was nice to me and wished me a 'Happy Christmas' before the school break.

But I was not ready for Mr Brodie's announcement.
'Well, you've been down there once already, haven't you?'

I nod yes.

'And you know the way?' Brodie asks.

It's not that I can't find it again. Of course I can.

'What? You can get food for birds but not birds for
food?'

It's not that either. It's the company.

'Then it's settled. You and Nell head down and pick
up the nicest goose you can get your hands on. The boys
have already brought back as many chickens as they could
carry. Get our goose and we're all set.'

So here I am walking through the snowy streets of
London with Nell.

'What do you think?' she says, after many quiet minutes.

'What do you mean?'

'A haircut. You fancy one?'

'Now?'

'No, not now, girl. Now we got food to collect. After
the holidays, say. I'll take you down to St Katharine Docks
myself.'

'Yes,' I say after a moment. 'OK. Thank you.'

In the winter dark, growers and traders sell their goods
by small oil lamps. Nobody really seems to notice how
beautiful Nell is. We get the goose quickly enough and
dash back through the cold. I still feel a bit second hand
around her, but now we are nearly friends.

Flo would be so jealous. I keep thinking about my new

haircut. All the girls wear their hair in curls now. Can I wear mine in curls? I would give anything to have hair like that. *Like Mum's.*

A man in an overcoat stands outside the twin-towered West Gate.

He is not the German, I can tell that straight away. I like the sight of him only slightly more.

He turns at our footsteps, fingers itching towards his camera.

'Hiya, girls,' he calls. 'Happy Christmas to you both. You two live in the Tower, do you?'

Neither of us answers, and I follow as Nell walks on.

'Just a quick question, nothing to be alarmed about.' He moves to stand before us. 'About the other residents of the Tower. I'm with the paper, you see? The people want to know how the ravens are doing. You know, all this business about some old Tower legend. Folks want to know if the birds are fit and healthy and all.'

'Of course,' I say, hoisting the giant goose as we pass. 'Just bringing them their Christmas meal now.'

The Watchman senses some disturbance and steps out of the Gatehouse. The photographer slinks away. But I am smiling. Uncle Henry didn't make up the legend of the ravens. Even the newspapers know about it. I ignore the voice in the back of my head that whispers, *you* told Churchill. Timothy Squire is the rotten liar, not Uncle.

At dinner, the table is covered in a cloth embroidered with red flowers. We have goose and roast potatoes, with cabbage from the allotment. The Stone Kitchen looks positively festive, with paper chains and sprigs of holly decorating the ceiling (no paper hats, though). For pudding, we are each given half a fig. Nuts are still scarce and dear, so we don't have those.

We open presents before the fire. My pillowcase is here in place of a stocking, and there is something inside – it is heavy. Has someone gone to Oxford Street? Uncle has given me a book (*The Sword in the Stone*), which I have read a million times. I smile and thank him.

From Oakes there is a card. It is only a card – no present – but with a quite lovely decoration of a robin on it. Inside it says *A Happy Christmas*. I mutter my thanks.

We sit listening to the wireless, carols from a college chapel (exact location censored – likely Cambridge). 'Star of Bethlehem' plays with Brodie's deep hum as accompaniment.

Back in my room, I write a card to Florence. I wish I could send it; I wish I knew where exactly she was.

A knock.

'Come in.' Strange for Uncle to visit at so late an hour. I wait another moment before calling in a louder voice.

'Come in!'

No one comes.

Quietly, I get up and push the door open. Nobody is there. But something is. Even though it is not wrapped, I know it is a present. A bit too small, the pages not lined; it is perfect.

A new workbook, with the name already filled in, in small, neat letters. *Magpie.*

A note inside.

I bought this for you – sod the paper ration.
I'm sorry. T.S.

Wednesday, 25 December 1940

The parade is at 9.50 a.m. outside the King's House. Again the Warders are in full red and gold dress, with their medals and ribbons proudly displayed. Sir Claud carries a staff with an enormous head, and Sparks, the Gaoler, carries an axe.

I think of Mum, and when we saw the Coronation together. Well, the Coronation parade, at any rate. Mum took me to see all the royals pass along Regent's Street. Three summers ago, though it feels like ten.

They even filmed it, and broadcast it all over. People covering the sidewalks and hanging out of the windows, cheering as the lines of soldiers and horses passed – the glittering uniforms and plumes, the wailing trumpets and bugles, the screeching pipes and drums – all leading the royal buggy on its way down Oxford Street, into Hyde Park, and to the palace.

Mum gripped my hand, told me who was who – the Canadian mounted police, the Colonials, the royal princesses – and she cheered loudly with everyone else. I remember her cheering anyway, even if I can't quite picture it now. She always liked the Duke of York, and was happy that he was going to be King.

Staring at Uncle, the parade of the past in my thoughts, the words just come.

'I don't remember,' I am saying. 'I just... don't. I'm *sure* I saw her, I always saw her before I left for school. She would make porridge, on the mornings she didn't have to go in early. Other days she walked me right to the bus stop, waving as I pulled away.'

I stop, look down at the dark stone.

'I don't remember *that* morning. If she was there, in the doorway, or at the bus stop, or already gone...'

Uncle leans forward, places a hand on my arm. The Warders march on, and we watch in silence.

Timothy Squire is there. His eyes, freed from the irritating brick dust, are not grey but a surprising blue. He keeps up his smile.

'Thank you for the gift,' I say, before turning back to the parade.

At Chapel the choir is smaller now, yet the voices seem louder. It is a short sermon: we must pray for peace, but peace is impossible until there is goodwill between men. I try to listen, to believe it, my eyes on the tall Christmas tree in the corner.

At home, our tree was always left up until New Year's Day, when Mum and I put it outside. All day the street would be lined with trees, still green while the real street trees were dead and empty of leaves for the winter. Even after the truck came to collect them, little needles littered the drive, shards of green in the white snow.

I stare around at the flagstone graves and memorials that fill the cold, white room. Buried underneath are Anne Boleyn, Catherine Howard, Lady Jane Grey, Sir Thomas More. 'Residents are baptized, married and buried at the Chapel,' the Chaplain once said.

Will I be buried here?

The sermon is over, and the choir sings again. I look back up at the stained-glass windows, thinking of the horrors of the slow-passing year.

Oh, God. Don't let me be that frightened ever again.

We were promised it would happen, yet to hear it now is astonishing. Church bells ring throughout the city. An incredible sound – the signal of death now the signal of hope. As the voices rise in 'When Shepherds Watched', tears fall from every eye.

I walk through the snow-dusted Green.

Grip careens into view, intent on his own business. Mabel, at least, would visit. She would examine you, nod in greeting, before moving on. I can still see him, though, and, wet from the earlier snowfall, I can detect the strong, almost fragrant smell of wet feathers, and it feels like I am sharing some of Christmas with Grip. I added some of my goose to his feeding (a bigger than palm-size slice) and he devoured it with obvious pleasure.

It is my duty to protect them. *To protect us.*

Always there have been ravens at the Tower.

We too are like the ravens. Maybe Timothy Squire isn't so wrong. We *have* become animals in order to survive: animals and thieves.

The houses were empty. Who are we leaving the food for? Rats?

I am so mad at him. I can scarcely think of that giant head without wanting to throw something at it. He doesn't understand anything. He doesn't *see.* How horrible it is.

To have another thing to lose.

'Hear that?' Uncle says, pointing at the wireless. 'The bells of the Coventry Cathedral. What remains of it.'

Christmas Day lunch was happy. Chips, beans, mince pie, a glass of port. I could have asked for nothing better. Osborne biscuits too.

Last Christmas, I went to the pantomime with Mum. Different from the other years, when Mrs Morgan came too. Rumour is that only one pantomime is showing in the West End – *Aladdin* – and the show times are strange – 12 noon and 4 p.m – in case the raids begin again.

We, of course, are staying in the Tower. An afternoon programme called *Christmas Under Fire* is on, and, along with the bells of Coventry Cathedral, there are interviews from troops in Iceland, Egypt, Bethlehem. Civilians in the country, in shelters, in the Underground, sing 'Good King Wenceslas'. Then, of course, the King himself speaks. For days Uncle has been readying us for this moment, his excitement almost enough to make him seem healthy again.

The radio voice, if occasionally halting, is clear enough:

Remember this: if war brings separation, it brings new unity also, a unity which comes from common perils and common sufferings, willingly shared. To be comrades and good neighbours in trouble is one of the finest opportunities of the civilian population.

It all happens like a kind of dream.

Another lovely dinner (though there are never onions any more), with Christmas pudding and mince pies. It is just nice to be almost warm inside, away from the dark windows and frost. To forget about bombers hunting the skies. Someone has even found a red tablecloth.

Uncle stands, and we all raise a glass.

'To our friends and families in the forces. To absent friends.'

'To absent friends,' we all repeat.

Everyone knows someone who is missing. Maybe prisoner, maybe killed. But then we smile, all of us, like in a play.

The fire is not quite enough to keep out the cold, which gnaws at my face and hands. Still I am smiling. Oakes, wearing blue overalls and a steel helmet, goes off to his night shift at the cathedral. Because of what happened in Coventry, people are volunteering to spend one night each week in St Paul's, equipped with water and sandbags. I am almost sad to see him go. *If I was wrong about him, could I be wrong about Timothy Squire, too?*

I am ready for bed, my stomach heavy and full, and I feel almost ready to laugh.

The little book of poems of course I no longer have. Father gave it to me for Christmas, when I was five. I don't remember that day – any more than I remember Father. Closing my old diary, I open the new one given to me by Timothy Squire, and briskly smooth the page. Without thinking, I begin to write:

> *I wandered lonely as a cloud*
> *That floats on high o'er vales and hills,*
> *When all at once i saw a crowd,*
> *A host, of golden daffodils;*

Beside the lake, beneath the trees,
Fluttering and dancing in the breeze.

There is more, but I can't think of it now. It is far too cold to believe in daffodils. With a little shock, I realize I am crying.

Maybe the siren will sound. When I peek through the curtain, up at the night sky, the stars are out again. Some bright, others dim, all scattered across the darkness. We are like that, Flo. Mabel. Mum. Father. Scattered like the stars.

Friday, 27 December 1940

Snow falls softly at mid-afternoon. It is a light snow and none of it has settled since Christmas. No footprints.

'All right, Anna?' says Timothy Squire uncertainly.

'Hello.'

'Happy Christmas.'

'Happy Christmas,' I say, walking on.

'Anna.'

Timothy Squire has caught up to me. 'Anna, I was just wondering... if, you know, you'd be up for a game? In the study, I mean.'

For a moment, under the drifting snow, I stand motionless. I shrug.

He laughs. 'I wasn't sure. You seemed so mad at me.'

'"Mad"?'

'Yeah.' He turns red. 'I mean, I know looting is wrong, but... you got *so* mad.'

'You don't understand anything.'

We are silent. I shiver, frowning into the distance. The wind has shifted.

'So,' he says after a moment, 'do you want to play?'

Again I shrug.

Over a shared Thermos of tea, Timothy Squire and I play Monopoly. He rubs his hair, makes lots of 'ooohs' and 'ahhhs', and says he got sent to gaol when I can see the card says *Second place in a beauty contest.*

He is lucky not to be in a real gaol.

The door opens and Leslie walks in, stopping when she sees us.

'Leslie,' I say, as Timothy Squire has disappeared into his usual silence around other people. Then I remember all the mean songs. 'Do you want to play?'

She looks down at the board with a twist of her lips. I realize that she is fighting off a smile. And not a nasty one.

'Nah, I'll leave you lovebirds to it.'

As she turns to go she abandons the fight, flashing a huge grin. My face is hot.

Timothy Squire hands me the dice, his expression nervous. He is different. Everything is different. In the early dusk the room seems dark, as though it has no walls, and just goes on and on forever. I roll – a ten – and I move the silver dog round the board.

He is quiet until his turn. 'I'm sorry, by the way. About whatever I said. People say all sorts of rubbish.'

'It's my turn,' I say, reaching for the dice.

'Do you want any help with the ravens?' Timothy Squire asks, looking at me from the corner of his eyes.

'"Help"?'

He quickly looks down at the board again. 'I mean... Can I come along? I'll help if I can.'

'Maybe,' I say after a moment's pause. I swallow a nasty comment about looting – and an apology about MacDonald. 'Let's finish the game first.'

Timothy Squire, nodding agreeably, carries on grousing about Headmaster Brownbill. I roll the dice again, smiling.

Saturday, 28 December 1940

The Christmas Truce is over. Free of the cloud banks, the moon is bright and huge. A full moon used to be called a Hunter's Moon, or Farmer's Moon – now it's a Bomber's Moon. The Germans have come early.

Already the Victoria and Albert Docks are burning. Hundreds of bombs fall all around, before the siren has even wailed. I must get to the shelter. But all I can think of are the faces, the panic, the uncertainty. No. I am not going underground.

I run instead to the tavern. People are there, Warders and curators, gathered round the wireless. Something in their faces forces me to stop, listen. It is the BBC broadcast.

Tonight the bombers of the German Reich hit London where it hurts the most, in her heart. St Paul's Cathedral, built by Sir Christopher Wren, her great dome towering over the capital of the Empire, is burning to the ground as I talk to you now.

Soon I am on the battlements, climbing, climbing. I can see it, wreathed in filthy, grey smoke.

Oakes. Everywhere he goes becomes a target. *Why didn't I tell Uncle about the German?* Oh, God, now it is too late.

Another thought, just as hopeless. Where is Uncle now?

I do not move. I watch and watch, for minutes, for hours, my eyes blinking but the sight remaining. Everything burns, a massive, seamless wall of fire. And there, right in the middle of it all, the Thames, *the river*, roaring with flames.

As the White Tower is hit I finally turn away. At least three incendiary bombs tear through the roof of the Main Guard building. The heavy walls crumble. No fire rises at first – maybe the incendiaries burned themselves out. Only smoke, drifting as if from Nell's cigarette. Then flames appear, fanned into life. The fire, whipped up by its own winds, grows and grows. Sparks fall like hail, driving down on us, starting new fires.

The stone is red in the reflected glow, playing across the

towers, winking at the turrets. It is out of control. The air itself scorches. The Germans are trying to burn the Tower down to its roots.

A noise, strange. The All Clear.

People emerge from the shelters. Miss Breedon, Yeoman Brodie, Headmaster Brownbill. Uncle, limping, yet very much alive. No one speaks. Up in the sky, snow is falling. Slowly – thick, heavy snow that vanishes long before it reaches us. The air is like a furnace.

I must go to check on Grip. A bomb landed just by the roost. The White Tower is wreathed in smoke; the Main Guard is completely destroyed. Everywhere is red. I must go.

But the London Fire Brigade has arrived, and nobody is to move.

The planes will return. You can see it on every face. Any moment, the siren will wail again. Somewhere stone collapses. *Who will bury us in the Chapel if we are all dead?*

A stretcher party arrives, *SP* on their helmets. Nurses too. The Heavy Rescue Team.

'No smoking,' says Yeoman Brodie, his voice short and angry.

'My mask,' I say suddenly. It's in my room.

'No use here,' Mr Brodie says grimly. 'This here is domestic gas. Just no smoking.'

I nod, absently scanning the distance for Nell. She is not there. Should she appear, the second she tries to light a match, I will stop her. Somehow.

'Over here, sir,' a man calls.

Mr Brodie and the rescue team gather round the rubble. Someone is in there. Kate, I can see. It is Kate.

'Well, get her out,' growls Mr Brodie.

A nurse turns on a shaded blue light. They lean over her. Shovels lift the scorched wood, the bright grey ash. Nurses are talking to Mr Brodie. One takes something from her bag – lipstick? – and leans over Kate. I strain to see, and when the nurse stands I can make out, printed across Kate's forehead, the letter 'M'. Her small body is lifted carefully on to a white stretcher.

While the others are talking quietly, I push forward.

'Ma'am.' I stop in front of the nurse, all but pulling on her sleeve. 'What does that mean? That letter you put on her?'

The face that greets me is shockingly old, grey and tired. 'It's for the hospital, dear. Your friend will be fine.'

'What does it mean? What does "M" mean?'

'Morphia,' she says, her voice expressionless. 'We've run out of tags. She'll be fine.'

What does she need morphia for? The question remains in my head, as the nurse has already trudged away, Kate in her stretcher not far behind.

Still the fires burn.

Another body. A girl from school, I can't tell. And then I see.

Leslie. She is quiet, unmoving. It is not a severed leg or a hanging foot as she always talked about. Just a girl lying still, turned softly to the side, her legs pale but free of blood or ash. She might be asleep. *She is not.*

Again the men yell for everyone to clear out, and again no one stirs. Brodie stands, his face turning red, turning angry.

'Stretcher,' he calls out. 'And a blanket. Now, move.'

It is brought and he leans down, still not touching her.

'It's all right, dear,' he says, his voice low. 'It's all right.' *Leslie.*

Above, snow falls. Still it does not reach us. Still the fires burn.

V

AT TRAITORS' GATE

Cheese not Churchill.

– Graffiti, East London

11

Saturday, 26 April 1941

Grip perches atop the curtain wall. Gusting winds carry the echo of winter. But winter is gone.

From 11 January no bombs fell, then a few sporadic attacks, and then nothing for a month. A massive raid on Saturday, 19 April, and now silence again. St Paul's, of course, was saved. Oakes is full of stories of the bravery of the Watch, his own included. I have my doubts.

After Leslie's funeral, things were sad. Her mother, Mrs Ballard, who I am ashamed to admit I once thought looked horsey, never stopped crying. Leslie's father, who serves in the army, got leave to come to the funeral and stayed on for several days. Both were crying when he left again. Normal life, though, is returning. Days whistle by. Oakes slurps his tea, stares at his wall. Nell really did take me for a haircut near St Katharine Docks – far too short, though it has since grown out much better. She even took me to Austin Reed and helped me find summer frocks.

(Uncle gave me some 'walking around money'.)

She is a *typist*, it turns out, when she's not the world's most absent firewatcher. What she types exactly, and for whom, remains a mystery. She asked if I had my monthlies coming on yet: I do *not* – but said I would tell her when I did. It sounds *horrible*, and I hope it never comes, even if it does give me a reason to visit Nell.

Even though I have not talked to her much since, she often smiles at me, or says 'looking snappy', to which I often say the wrong thing or forget to say anything at all.

When I see her today, she is carrying a bag. A large bag, and full. I ask, politely yet casually, where she is going.

'Leaving,' she says.

'What? But you… you're an East Ender.'

Her laughter, so unlike her voice, is high and clear. 'I am that, dear. That is true enough. But I'm not moving house.'

'Where are you going?'

She shrugs. 'Called up. WVS needs help.'

I try not to imagine just how ill-suited Nell is for the work. And she is gone.

Will conscription extend to all women? To girls? I know lots of women have been working in the munitions factories – Leslie once told me all about it. It sounds horribly hard and dirty. Will we be called up now?

Things with Timothy Squire seem to be getting back to normal too. I haven't seen him much – we still start the odd game of Monopoly (he always 'lets' me use the silver dog), or sit around and talk about nothing in particular.

Once or twice he helped with the ravens. He even turned round to smile at me in class one day. I coughed and looked away.

Soon this will all change. I cannot be mad at him forever.

'Come on then,' he will say, 'I was waiting for us to be friends again.' Then we will walk along the battlements, go back to the market and smell the baking bread. When the sun gets warmer, we will visit the beach and have a swim, the water not cold but deliciously cool. Timothy Squire likely isn't a strong swimmer. He'll be able to paddle out to where I am. Then I will show him how to kick his feet properly. *The sea is a dangerous place.*

I do miss him being around, how he always seems to be enjoying life tremendously. Perhaps I was too hard on him. He can't be himself. Not in war, not in *this*.

No one acts like they truly are.

A troop of the Scots Guard has arrived and moved into the barracks; they have turned the Tower into a party. Dances, concerts, pub nights. They bring their girls inside – all of them scented and made-up, with handbags and gas masks – and make all kinds of racket. I thought that I would welcome some life in this place. Something about the new soldiers, though – the *attitude* – feels out of place.

I have glanced in through the windows (the Tudor Room has been cleared) when they're all dancing. Fast waltzes, lots of stepping and twisting, and always a Highland reel with the screeching bagpipes.

Uncle called it a 'permanent' garrison, which means I'll have to get used to seven companies of Scots Guards and their parties. Some of us have to study. Final examinations before school reports are barely a week away. Already I fear Uncle's disappointment upon learning that the perfect lamb is not at all a satisfactory student.

After next year when I leave school, maybe I will join the NAAFI girls. Some are as young as fourteen, and they seem happy enough. After a few weeks of work I can save up enough money to book a seat on a steamer. It will be a scary journey – many days and nights – before I arrive in Montreal.

First things first.

I must meet Kate and begin studying. She is now back from the hospital and considerably less horrid. We don't talk about Leslie a lot, how much we both miss her wild stories and her eye rolling. Headmaster Brownbill remains as mean as ever, glaring at us with his hard stare.

If Timothy Squire wanted to apologize properly – for *everything* rotten he has done – well then, he would. I may avoid seeing him most of the time, but he can *find* me if he wants to. He can find bloody shrapnel in the streets.

The rain will come, I know now, and spring will be no different from winter. *Rain clears the air,* Mum used to say. The thought of Mum talking to me makes all my examination study slip from my mind.

I open my book: 239 days since the first raid. A lifetime.

I am safe here. That is what Mum would have wanted, me safe.

From behind me comes a strangled cry. Voices, screaming. I race back down the stairs, on to the Green.

'Look at them! I know – I can see the evil. They terrify everyone. No more.'

Warders have gathered alongside the confused looking Scots Guard. I push forward, catching a glimpse of Uncle in the middle of the circle. Someone is yelling at him.

'They help the bombers. They want us dead.'

The deep voice is familiar; I need to come to the edge to be sure. I watch with wide eyes. Yeoman Brodie is roaring at Uncle. *What is going on?*

A flash of metal. Brodie has a knife. And in his other hand Mr Brodie holds Raven Grip.

'They are evil. Can't you see it? My son is terrified of them. I've had enough, Henry. It's them or us!'

I stare in disbelief. *Yeoman Brodie, with his almost crooked nose and his stories about the Tower. How could you?*

Uncle moves faster than I could imagine, pulling the raven free from the giant man's grasp. Grip, feathers ruffled, marches indignantly away.

Brodie, snarling, continues to yell in his ringing voice.

'They will get us all killed!'

Uncle shouts too, his voice thick and angry, but wary of the larger man wielding a knife. 'What is the matter with you? Bloody fool.'

Malcolm appears from beyond the Chapel, running to his father's side. I grab his arm as he flies past, holding him still. He tries to lurch free, but I am stronger.

'Let me go!' he cries, vicious.

'Hold on,' I say, keeping my voice calm. 'Just hold on, Malcolm.'

Malcolm squirms and mutters, but puts up little fight. My voice is calm but I am not. I can only stare at Yeoman Brodie, the kind, smiling giant from breakfast. *He killed MacDonald. I can't believe it.*

Brodie stares back, seeing his son. He lets the knife drop to the stone. Uncle reaches down and picks it up, slipping it into his belt.

'Go get some rest, Yeoman Brodie.'

Brodie still does not move. I let go of Malcolm's arm and he races to his father. Brodie grips his shoulder, gives a sad smile.

'Come on, son. Let's go home.'

Dazed, the two walk together back to the barracks.

Sunday, 4 May 1941

The light stays until 10 p.m. Well, the new 10 p.m. anyway. Someone has decided to change the clocks. 'Double

Summer Time' means putting the clocks ahead two hours. I imagine they think we've earned it.

Which means the return of regular sleeping patterns. It also means the extended daytime for Grip. A bird of habit, he returns every night by exactly the same route. *I essentially wait for him.*

Grip has other worries. Stirred by the coming spring, he has begun to behave erratically, obsessively. He marches, chest puffed, carrying sticks and foil from cigarette packs. He is nesting. Anything found or stolen is put to use: paper, grass, clumps of mud.

Male ravens don't build the nest – and of course he won't lay eggs. Still he carries sticks and twigs behind the crumbling curtain wall. *It is not a choice.* I realize the truth of Uncle's words as I watch Grip. It is something beyond his control. He has *changed* with the new season.

I can't help but think of Mabel, somewhere in the city. Is she building a nest out there, high in a tree? Eating meals whenever she wants, noon picnics and midnight feasts? Or will she finally return to help, so she and Grip can build a nest together?

The spring has changed us too. I feel the pleasant sting of a day in the sun, the tightness in my face. A new bloom of freckles; I don't care what anyone thinks. The sky is huge, and almost perfectly blue.

What happened to Yeoman Brodie, nobody will say for certain. He has not been at breakfast since that morning. Malcolm, though, I still see slinking around, with his mother glued to his side. *I have seen her more times this morning than I have since I've been here.*

Uncle says that Brodie has gone to the countryside to rest. For how long? He killed MacDonald and tried to kill Grip. What happens when he returns?

'War is hard on us all,' was all Uncle said. Something in his eyes gives him away. *He is not telling me everything.*

No one tells me the truth. I know that now. But I too have changed.

Timothy Squire and his NAFFI girl. I see them walking together. She is *years* older than him, at least fifteen or sixteen. I can see that he is telling one of his stupid bomb stories.

So this is why he never talks to me any more.

I think of my old form teacher, Miss Woodside. I remember with a hollow stomach how, directly after prayers, she once told all the students – not just the fifth- and sixth-form girls – to go into the music room. There she droned on about 'the dangers of lowering morals in wartime'.

I looked at the other second-form girls, mystified, because it didn't concern us at all – people going to bed who are not married. (Flo had already told us that her mum said that war would make London 'a paved double bed'.) The others squirmed too, having heard it all. But

Miss Woodside still savaged on about it. Of course, Tower School is a boys' and girls' school so they would never have such talks here.

The NAAFI girl is laughing, laughing in her stupid hat. And Timothy Squire in his. Or whoever's hat it was before he stole it. I wonder how long it took to find one big enough for his head. Who would ever want to be a NAAFI girl – the stupid outfit, making food all day for the soldiers? It sounds awful.

'Timothy Squire,' I call.

He waves, but does not move from the NAAFI girl's side. Her lips are red. Too red. *Of course, that lipstick he stole.*

I raise my voice louder. 'Don't be an idiot, Timothy Squire. Come here. It's important.'

This seems to give him pause, and after a brief and obviously ridiculous exchange between them, Timothy Squire approaches. NAAFI girl wanders off towards the White Tower.

'What's important?' he tries to give his old smile; it just looks foolish.

'What else – besides canteen girls – do you care about?' I smile back. 'Bombs.'

He lets the first remark go in his excitement for the second. 'What kind?'

'You tell me. I need to know something – about a certain type of bomb. I've been looking, but I haven't been able to figure out exactly how it works.'

'You should've asked me.'

'Well, I'm asking you now.'

We stand in silence on the Green. He looks up at me, waiting.

'It's about a bomb they haven't dropped yet,' I say. 'But everyone always talks about it. Poison. The gas bomb.'

He looks at me strangely. 'Yes?'

'How does it... kill? The gas bomb. How does it kill?'

He looks at me, nervous, thinking. 'It is... the gas stops your breathing. So you die.'

We look at each other for a moment. I remember all the things he said. *We all do what we must.* It is cool in the dusk and soon we both grow still. He does not look away, but nods very slowly before speaking.

'Like going to sleep.'

I nod, turning my face towards the now sinking sun.

Saturday, 10 May 1941

'Uncle, I need to talk to you.'

'And I need to talk to *you*. Come, dear.'

He is in unusually good spirits today. Perhaps I can finally get him to answer me honestly. But first things first.

'No, no,' he says, seeing me reach for the gloves. 'The birds can take care of themselves today. We're going out.'

I stare at him, no words coming. Dazzling light streams

in through the stained glass. Finally, I manage a cracked, 'Where?'

He grins, a rakish gleam in his eye. He looks almost flushed. 'Where else? Wembley.'

I nod dumbly, unsure what to make of his transformation.

Wembley?

We walk out in the cold. Uncle wears a brown suit and a trilby hat, limping slightly. I have changed into the new spring outfit Nell helped me pick out. Although the white jumper is hers (it is a little long at the arms), the navy skirt is straight from the shops. *Now I really look like a Magpie, glowing in the sun.* I smile at the thought but suddenly shiver. Maybe I should have worn my old trousers. Those blessed few days of warmth seem a different life ago. Is it really May?

It must be because buses now run on summer timetables. The driver punches our fourpenny tickets and we find seats as near as we can to the front. The air is stuffy, with an unpleasant smell like damp laundry. Green gauze is stretched tight across the windows. Out there is the city where I have spent my whole life, Which I may no longer recognize.

'What a match,' Uncle is saying. 'Preston won in nineteen thirty-eight. Haven't lost a game this year. But Arsenal is older, more experienced, and miserly with goals.'

While Uncle's enthusiasm has startled me, I have not forgotten my determination to get the truth.

The bus driver calls out: 'Sorry about the detour, folks. There's been a nasty old man in the sky dropping stones.'

A few low chuckles, Uncle among them.

'Did your mum ever tell you about the QPR games?' Uncle smiles widely. 'Oh, she loved them.'

There is nothing possible to say. Mum at a football match?

Uncle reads my expression clearly enough. 'Oh yes. Dad loved the Hoops, and we would beg him to bring us along to White City. Your mum too, though I fear her love was more particular. How she swooned over Harry Pidgeon!'

I feel my face go red. 'Who?'

'He could dribble up the field like a dancer. Scored the odd goal, as well. Your mum must have been around your age. I think her affection was quite serious.'

Uncle is laughing like I have never heard him before. He is too pleased for me to say what I want to – what kind of name is *Harry Pidgeon*? – so I just gaze round the strange green interior of the bus. I keep staring, tangled in thought. I don't mean to think it, I don't *want* to, but it is everywhere.

'Mum died on a bus like this.'

Although he goes very pale, he says nothing. After a moment, Uncle reaches over and squeezes my hand.

Despite my new resolution I can't bring myself to ask the question.

Didn't she?

When we get off the bus, the streets are humming like a beehive. I almost offer Uncle my arm, but he seems steady enough. Hawkers are selling red and white peonies and small Union Jack flags. Girls stand in summer dresses, despite the cold. I know Timothy Squire wishes he could be here.

'Isn't it dangerous?' I wonder aloud.

'No, no,' Uncle says. 'Perfectly safe.'

Perfectly safe? The sun glints off the shining faces as we march along. If there is a daytime raid, we'll be a perfect target. Another, slightly less terrifying thought grabs me. *How long is the game?* Surely we won't still be here after nightfall. Surely.

We are inside the stadium. *I am inside Wembley*: sixty thousand people in the cold sunshine, all staring towards the brilliant green pitch. Uncle looks so happy that I can't bring myself to ask anything more about Mum or the length of the match. His eagerness is infectious.

The game is set to begin at 3.30 p.m. A cheer rises up, and the players emerge from the tunnels. Uncle cheers too, and my heart surges to see him. *He looks like Mum now.* Mum when she would read me *The Hobbit*, doing all the different voices. Her voice for the dragon was low and scary, but she laughed, too.

The national anthem explodes into the arena. It is easy

to become dizzy amid all the roaring voices.

'See the young lad up front for Arsenal?' Uncle yells to be heard, pointing vaguely at players in red and white. 'Denis Compton. A sublime talent.'

I nod. This is almost as loud as a raid.

Preston in dark shorts looks like the slower team. Something happens – people are screaming – a penalty to Arsenal. The shot, hard and sure, is saved. Only three minutes gone. My legs are *frozen*.

Soon Uncle hands me my 'picnic' lunch of a cheese sandwich and crisps. Afterwards, though, I feel a little queasy. I adjust my positioning, stretching my legs in the light.

Now Preston moves faster. The post rattles. Another shot, and Preston scores. Uncle looks tired, but is always smiling. Happy. Just before half-time, Arsenal scores and the game is tied. Five clouds hang in the sky.

Although the players looked exhausted in the second half, the crowd cries with the same enthusiasm, even Uncle. The game goes on for a very long time, the ball kicked back and forth. Eventually, it ends in a draw. They will have to play again to settle on a winner. I make a note to tell Uncle that examinations are coming up and I'm really not feeling that prepared. *That is only half a lie.*

It is 5 p.m., beautiful and sunny and freezing. Even though I move as quickly as I can, the crowd is in no hurry to leave the stadium. Once we reach the gates, the pace is slower than Grip waddling to the roost for bed. I pause, knuckling my back, before lumbering long with the laughing figures.

'Our day is not over,' Uncle looks down at me with a wink.

'Oh, Uncle. I have had the most glorious day. I can't thank you enough. But I would really rather just enjoy the sunshine – maybe wander around London a bit.'

'Oh no, dear. You will not want to miss this.'

Uncle may be wrong. As another bus winds through the invisible streets, we sit in silence. Kate told me that the police have agreed to a new closing time, and cinemas and pubs are now open until 10 p.m. Uncle can't plan to be out for so long, can he? I glance at him now. He looks older, worn, hidden under a hat.

Once we're off the bus, we stop for tea and scones, which are delicious, and then Uncle checks his watch and says we have to hurry. When we finally turn and walk up to the Queen's Hall, I cannot raise a smile.

'A concert,' I say, straining to keep the disappointment from my voice.

'Oh no,' he answers, not looking down. 'Elgar's masterpiece.'

Of course, once we get inside and take our seats, it turns out to be very much a concert. '*The Dream of*

Gerontius,' Uncle says, assuming perhaps that I am familiar with Gerontius. He makes various noises about Mum,
how pleased she would be if she could see us.

The room, though, is quite splendid, and the fancy
musicians and singers fill the stage. I wonder, and not
for the first time, if Uncle truly had me in mind when he
bought these tickets. Football and concerts? Is Oakes on
duty at St Paul's tonight?

When Mum took me out for a birthday treat, she
always *asked* what I wanted to eat. Even if we couldn't
have it, she'd find us something similar.

The music is long and dull. My legs are sore from the
day of sitting in the cold, and it is a shock to go from the
screaming openness of the football to the quiet unmoving
stiffness of the concert hall. My mind drifts to Monopoly.
My little silver dog, moving along the board. Timothy
Squire, laughing and talking. Not doing anything evil or
horrible.

*It's not Timothy Squire's fault. It's the war. We are not
ourselves.*

No. If we are not ourselves now, when things are
hardest, when we are needed most, when are we? Is this
our best, lying and stealing? Running away and abandon-
ing those we love? To this? To this world without them? I
realize with a jolt that I am no longer thinking of Timothy
Squire.

'Your mother was very talented, as you must know,'
comes a piercing whisper, 'a fine violinist. Listen, listen.'

Uncle is doing his thing where he is talking, but not really *to* anyone. 'This part... here.' And, after a moment, 'Oh, I'm sure she *loved* this piece.'

Uncle is too far away to notice my sour look. Mum told me herself she wasn't good enough to play professionally for a living, though she would sit for hours in her study with her violin, and forget to come out even to say goodnight. In the later days, she didn't play the violin so much. Still she went into her study, the brown wooden door closed tight. Father, she said, had been a truly gifted violinist. If I ever heard him play, I don't remember it.

While there is much church singing, eventually the noisy voices and strings do come together quite beautifully. Perhaps Mum *would* have been pleased to see me here.

The night air is freezing but welcome. I take a huge gulp of it. I would rather be frozen outside than stuffed in some fancy room with old people who do nothing but cough. *No one even clapped until the very end.* Never have I seen a moon so bright.

It is a quiet bus ride home. Cold air seeps inside, and Uncle soon drifts to sleep. *I will have another chance to ask him.* Once we get home, however, the moment we are back inside the Tower, an old sound returns. I can't take my eyes from the barracks clock. It is 11.03 p.m. It has been three weeks.

The siren is wailing. At the time, it is a shock – the siren had been so quiet, and now my eardrums throb from the old, immediately familiar sound. But there is nothing in it to warn us that this was the night that Hitler had long been planning.

The night he would make us surrender.

Guns fire with the siren still in the air.

The British fighters are not in the sky yet. They are not in the sky when the first wave of German bombers passes over. Planes, countless planes, more than I have ever seen at once. They are not in the sky when the string of incendiaries lands on the Tower.

The east Casemates is hit. Constable Tower burns. Uncle says nothing. We have not moved from the grounds in front of the barracks. We stand, breathing heavily, looking out over the city. Between London Bridge and Southwark Bridge there is only a wall of flames. The moon, through the smoke, is still visible, high and bright and distant. I just keep swallowing, unable to stop myself.

No one goes to the shelter. No one moves. We are frozen, witnesses to these last moments, to this end.

It is nearly midnight. There comes a terrible rush of wind. Still we do not move. Oakes runs out, clearly searching for us, before joining our motionless vigil. I am too terrified to even move away from him.

An unknown amount of time passes, and the city is

destroyed. Fire rains from the sky. Torches rise from the city to greet it. Everything is lit, the flames beacons for further destruction. The fire's own wind churns up glass and sparks.

Below us roars a huge semicircle of fires. London bubbles and smokes, like a pot of boiling stew. I forget about everything. About Mum, about Father, about Timothy Squire, about Cora and MacDonald, about Oakes and the German.

The air is filled with debris. Everything is confused – I don't know how I am standing or if I even am. The cold stone is beneath me and above me, and the world is ringing and pulsing. Even the moon is gone now. Dust fills my nose, my mouth.

The Tower breathes fire. Smoke drills flit through my mind – *crawl on your stomach, mouth as near the floor as possible* – still I don't move. The wall of flames hems us in.

Another incendiary lands: to see it, just there. It is smaller than I thought it would be, smaller than Timothy Squire had me believe. He is a rotten liar. It is tiny, malicious, hissing. What happens when it ignites? I have always wondered. Will the world turn black? Disappear? Will I feel the heat on my skin?

All around me, people run. I see, though, in the distance, on the other side of the Tower, the dark outline of a figure on the ground. I can tell from the size and shape that it is Malcolm. Not ten feet from the white sputter of the bomb.

Without thinking, I move to the sandbags and pull one free. Someone screams my name. The sandbag is heavy, almost heavy enough to pull me over. Instead I stagger ahead. A hand reaches for me; I shoulder it away.

I can feel the heat of the bomb. It is too hot. What did Timothy Squire say? *It will cool.* I have no time to wait. I trudge into the wall of heat, dragging the sandbag behind me. I can hear nothing other than the rumble of the planes and the mocking whir of the bomb.

There is Malcolm, hands over his face, lying far too close. *His father is not here. Yeoman Brodie is away, off in the countryside somewhere.* Any moment now the incendiary will roar to life, and we will be buried in the avalanche of stone turrets and the east wall. I think of Flo, running on and on, long after my own breath gave out and my legs felt strangely light and clumsy.

You can do this.

I see in my mind the large, black, watching eye of Grip. *I am sorry.*

I inch forward in the heat. There is no time. I wield the sandbag, but I miss the bomb by several feet. I am not close enough.

I move nearer, clenching the sandbag. Again I wield it, and this time I strike the hissing bomb. And again and again. I pummel the bomb to death. The sandbag is heavy now, too heavy to lift once more.

An arm pulls me, hard. Then I feel nothing except the blistering heat.

12

Tuesday, 13 May 1941

I am in bed. Somewhere much more comfortable than my creaking bunk. My arm is wrapped tightly in white cloth – another bedsheet, I notice – and the air smells heavily of iodine.

Hitting that bomb. I can still remember, I can still *feel* it, the exhilaration.

Thank you, Flo.

Uncle comes in. I beam at him. That he is so strong, so fast – that he raced into that blaze to save me. As I look at him, though, I can say none of these words. I can only smile up at his concerned expression.

He has brought eggs and toast, which I eat awkwardly with my left hand.

'It is good to see you awake and smiling, my dear,' he says. 'Two days, and you've barely woken up to have a sip of water.'

'I'm feeling better now, Uncle. Thank you.'

He smiles, a kind smile. 'You're looking fighting fit. In a few weeks your hair will have grown right back.'

'*My hair?*'

I try to reach up but my arm is wrapped too tight. With my left I explore, tentatively, the top of my head. There is *some* hair, at least, though not at all even. *I can't let Nell see me like this.* God, what will Timothy Squire say? In a few *weeks* it will grow back?

'Are you okay, dear? I hope so. Because there is someone who wants to see you, if you have the strength for visitors.'

Before I can even answer the door is opened. Awkwardly, Malcolm is ushered into the room by a red-faced nurse. I turn my head on the pillow, not sure which way to shift. *What does my hair look like?*

'Come on in, Malcolm. Is there anything you want to say to Anna?'

He shuffles closer. He looks more pained than I have ever seen him.

'Thank you,' he finally mutters.

I smile back at him. At least he recognizes me. *My hair can't be that bad.*

'Can I go now?' He turns helplessly to Uncle, who nods. Grip would have had more to say.

I am in the Hospital Block, I finally realize – I have never been in here before. I must get a mirror.

'And you,' Uncle says, touching me gently, 'owe a debt yourself. Gregory is at the cathedral this morning, but he should be back this afternoon.'

'Yeoman Oakes?' I say weakly.

'A very foolish thing to do, Anna, running into that fire. Luckily, Gregory was close enough to reach you. No one else could have.'

Oakes?

Uncle tells me more. He protests, says I am too tired, too sleepy; I ask until he tells me everything. Untold damage, thousands dead or dying. So many places were hit: the British Museum, Westminster Abbey, St Mary-le-Bow, Somerset House, King's Cross Station, Big Ben, and the House of Commons. The Queen's Hall, where only hours before we had sat listening to the music of Gerontius, has burned to ash. The moon, when it reappeared, shone red, reflecting the blazing streets below.

The two nights since have seen no attacks. Lucky for me, as I was apparently just lying here, under no shelter apart from these white sheets. No one thinks this is the end, not after nine months. What will it take? Life cannot continue. Not like this. We have done all we can. We can do no more.

But Uncle has other news. The school building in the Mint has been destroyed. School is cancelled for the year. I have no time to count my blessings – *no student report!* – as Uncle keeps talking. The mere fact that the building is rubble is not the only reason why school has been cut short.

'Many of the parents are worried, rightly, of course,' he says. His next words echo strangely in my ears. 'Some of the kids have been sent away.'

'Evacuated? Now?'

'Yes. Some to Gloucester, others north.'

My heart seizes. Flo has already been taken from me; poor Leslie was killed. If Kate leaves too...

'Malcolm is being sent to Gloucester to stay with his father. And Mavis's boy, Carson. Rosemary and Jill Parrett. And the Squire family.'

The world seems to move more slowly. Uncle is there, sitting beside the bed in his old suit and tie; I can't seem to piece it together. What is he saying?

'Mr Squire was so distraught. You should have heard him after Timothy ran from the shelter that night. Gregory had to hold him from running out into the bombing after his son. Now, with the latest attack... it was too much. He loves that boy. They had to go somewhere safe, the whole family. Timothy Squire had to go away, Anna dear.'

'When? When are they going?'

His face is drawn tight.

'Malcolm and Carson leave at noon, I believe. The others took yesterday's train.'

Sunday, 18 May 1941

Leslie's mum was nice enough to lend me a hat for Chapel. It is quite unbecoming, covered in fake blue flowers, and far too big, but at least no one can see my hair. I shall have to wear this hat for several more weeks.

Maybe by then Timothy Squire will have returned.

'Oh, my dear. When you asked me if Mr Squire's boy, if Timothy, had left anything for you, I thought... Well, I did find a curious thing, on the floor by the bed, but I thought one of the nurses must have dropped it...'

'What? Where is it?'

We are leaving Chapel along with all the others when he casually mentions *this*. Sparks says a jolly hello in passing but I don't even respond. I am surprised he noticed me, hiding under Mrs Ballard's hat.

Uncle looks taken aback. 'It is, ah, it's just here.'

For an eternity he rummages in the pocket of his brown suit, before handing me the small object.

'What is it?'

Uncle squints in the sunlight. 'I don't know. I thought perhaps you might know. I assumed it was nothing at first, a trifle left in this old suit, until I recalled where I picked it up. I had hoped, given the circumstances, that maybe it had some significance?'

None that I can see. What the bloody hell is it? Is it a joke?

It *looks* like a tiny piece of metal, the size of a thumb – a piece of a bomb, or shrapnel maybe? Then I see the weird shape at the base, almost like a...

'What happened to the study? The night of the May raid?'

Uncle shakes his head sadly. 'I am sorry, my dear. The study was destroyed along with the school.'

Not all of it, I think, putting the half-melted silver dog into the pocket of my dress. *Timothy Squire.*

Uncle has started walking again, giving up the mystery as lost. I keep pace, my face blank. In my pocket, though, I can feel the weight of the metal figure.

A final act of scavenging.

Wednesday, 21 May 1941

Everything is different now. I can walk without pain, some of my hair has grown back (but I am never without Mrs Ballard's hat), and the weather is warm and bright even as dusk falls. But things have not changed *this* much. Something very unusual is happening. Soldiers are acting oddly and extra Warders walk their beats. Everyone seems in a tizzy, the nurses and the NAAFI girls, women and men walking quickly, heads down.

I have seen it, spending the week sitting on the Green in the sun until Uncle fusses and sends me back to bed. I took the news of the others leaving poorly, I suppose.

Or is he trying to hide something from me?

Official word is that Hitler has given up on the raids. The unofficial word is that one more night like the last raid would have been the end. Kate says that Churchill was by the phone, ready to surrender. So what is happening now?

More guards are entering the Tower. Doing my best to look uninterested, I close my eyes and lean my face into the sunlight. I have spent the past few afternoons here alone. Grip scarcely leaves the roost now. Even if he is sick, at least he is unhurt. *Again you did nothing to try and save him.*

I saved Malcolm. But he is a boy, a human – a friend.

I open my eyes again to some new noise.

A Scots Guard comes up to me. He is tall and handsome, younger than any of the Warders. I smile up at him.

'You'd best get back inside.' His tone is stern.

'Uncle lets me stay until the two o'clock bell.'

In truth, Uncle wants me back inside by 1.30, but I must find out what is going on.

'Well, not today, love. Get back inside. On you go.'

He grabs me, not gently, and steers me away from the Green. I have no choice but to go. Before I turn the corner, though, I sneak a look back, and I can see, like a kicked ant-hill, Scots Guard soldiers swarming over the bridge. Getting ready.

For what?

I wait until nightfall to find out.

It is quiet, the usual cheers from the White Tower silenced. The Scots Guard must be taking a night off from their dances. Poised, watchful, they man the battlements and crowd the West Gate entrance.

I will not be locked away in my room. I will see what is happening. I will know the truth.

This is why Uncle gave me the dagger. It is dull, of course, the blade more suited to butter, if by some miracle butter should arrive. *It will keep you safe*, Uncle had said, realizing what was coming, that everyone in London should have a weapon of some kind. *The handle is of yew, the same wood as the longbows of the famous yeoman archers.* And then Churchill's voice, a low growl. *You can always take one with you.*

Dark clouds drift in the black air. Something catches my eye in the distance. I almost stand on my toes to see the figure, moving. I know it is Oakes – walking away from Traitors' Gate.

And he is not alone.

Oakes disappears back inside the Inner Ward; the other figure is still there.

Then the figure turns – I am sure of it – and walks deeper into the castle.

For a full minute I pause, my ears straining for every sound. Nothing except silence and the echoing wind.

There *was* a man, though. And I know where he was going.

I know the route so well that the darkness doesn't slow me.

One of the Scots Guard, unfamiliar with the Tower, briefly flicks on his lantern to orient himself. I stop. *Violet would give him an earful.* The war is not over and the blackout must still be maintained. My heart beats and beats. The soldier disappears.

Kraa.

A raven's call cracks the still air. Loud and unmistakable, it echoes across the Green. *I knew it.*

No. I stop my thoughts before they can run off. It is just a bird, calling as it always does.

But Grip should be asleep – he should have been asleep for hours now. Ravens are not like us; when it's time for sleep, they sleep. *And when the sun comes up, they are up.*

The night air feels suddenly colder. The croak does not come again, yet I am certain that I heard it. *Not the usual low gurgle. A harsher, grating call.* The warning.

Grip?

The last raven in the Tower of London.

Reaching the roost, I stop. Night and shadows surround me. I squint through the folds of blackness.

Someone is there, standing in front of the cages. It is not Uncle – or any Warder.

The spring wind turns cold. No, it is not a spy, or a Nazi come to kill Grip. It is a regular soldier, from the Scots Guard. A trick of my hungry, exhausted mind. A trick of this place.

I walk up and stand boldly before the figure.

'And who are you, miss?' comes a voice.

He *is* a soldier; I can just make out a uniform. He turns away before I can see his face.

What am I going to say? That I have Uncle's permission to be out? That I am the assistant Ravenmaster, and it is my responsibility to ensure that my bird sleeps through the night without disturbance? *I am a mad young girl in a too-big church hat.*

Slowly the figure walks – limping slightly – to Grip's cage, pausing before it. Good luck to him. Ravens are invisible in the dark.

The uniform, I can see now, is not of the Scots Guard. The figure does not look at me again, but now I am frightened. All at once my prepared speech vanishes from my thoughts. The voice, strange and guttural, speaks from the darkness.

'Do you have a name?'

I do not run. Something in me stirs, I adjust the brim of Mrs Ballard's hat, and I speak.

'I am Anna. The Ravenmaster.'

There is a pause, and when the voice resumes it is clearly pleased. It is English, though not as people normally speak it. *I have heard this accent before.*

'You care for the raven? He is quite majestic. Perhaps a little lonely.'

I nod, unsure whether or not the voice can see me. A cold feeling runs down my arms. Is it the same man – returned now in his uniform? *Oakes's friend?*

Turn round.

'You are the Nazi.'

The man steps into the moonlight. Tall, with dark bushy eyebrows, a firm jaw, and black hair with a shine matched only by the black of his eyes.

'I am a Nazi, yes.'

He bows, and in the silent night his heels click loudly to attention. The uniform I recognize clearly from the *Spot at Sight* posters all over the city. Before I can react, before I can run screaming from this dreadful Tower and the lies and the traitors, the voice speaks again.

'My name is Rudolf Hess. I am the Deputy Fuhrer of the Nazi Party.'

13

'What do you feed him?'

It takes me a moment to understand the question. To be so close to such evil. I stand still in the moonlight.

The Deputy Fuhrer of the Nazi Party. He is not lying, that much is obvious.

'Biscuits… and blood. Meat.'

He makes a pained face, holds his stomach. 'Meat is bad for the digestion.'

Orrk. Orrk.

Grip croaks as if in protest. We both turn at the sound. The bird cannot be seen. Only sounds, shuffling amid the branches, and low, gurgling croaks. He is not Grip, a single bird with a bad temper and a taste for chocolate. In the darkness, he is a raven – all ravens, every raven.

'Do not worry, Ravenmaster Anna. I mean no harm to your bird or your country.'

'Why are you here?'

He stares down into the cage for another moment and then looks up to the sky. The voice continues, slow and cavernous, suited to the ancient stone around us.

'I had a dream, several months ago. A dream where I flew to Great Britain and stopped this wasteful war. I am Hitler's second-in-command. You see that I am the only one who could do it? I knew it too.'

'Oakes let you in?'

He looks at me with a sad smile. 'I came as an ambassador. An ambassador for peace.'

'But… you are a Nazi.'

He is smiling now, and his eyes shine even brighter. 'You must never ignore your dreams, Anna the Ravenmaster. I was walking, with footsteps that echoed all around me, through the halls of an ancient English castle, bringing peace between nations. They think I am a prisoner, but I was *meant* to come here.'

It is a trick. I know at once. *He knows about the prophecy. Oakes has told him. Without the Tower ravens, the kingdom will fall.*

He is here to kill Grip.

He is staring at me. His eyes are not unkind, yet something in them makes me shiver.

Where are the guards? I am suddenly aware of the knife in my jacket. If he opens the roost, can I stop him? Where is Uncle – or Sparks?

I saved Grip from bombs and starvation. I can save Grip from you.

Churchill's voice returns, slow and deliberate. *You can always take one with you.*

'All of your allies have surrendered. France, Belgium, Holland, Norway, Denmark, Poland. Our army is three times the size of yours. But the English are an intelligent, sympathetic people,' Hess is saying. 'Peace parties exist here. There is a real war that must be fought, but it is not between Great Britain and Germany.'

I think only of the knife in my coat. *The moment he opens the cage.*

'Your father is a soldier?'

My hand itches. 'My father is dead. My mother was killed by the Nazis.'

He stares at me for a moment. 'War killed your mother. War that Churchill wants to continue. That is why I came. That is why I sacrificed everything – my position, my family, my life, my country. That is why. For peace.'

He is lying, of course, his twisted German mind trying to manipulate me, to force me to listen. I do not let my hand drop.

'You do not believe me,' he says after a moment. 'I do not blame you. Maybe no one will listen. But still, I had to. Don't you see? But here. Take this. I see that my guards are coming for me again.'

I hear it too, now, the men approaching. Oakes is among them. Hess takes a folded piece of paper from his pocket. With a trembling hand I reach out. I take it.

The guards are nearly here.

'It is in English. A poem I wrote, long ago. Good luck with your bird, Ravenmaster Anna.'

I step back into the shadows, and Oakes and two Scots Guards appear and direct him back to the King's House without a glance towards me. In the darkness the clacking of my teeth is the only sound.

'Uncle, I am so sorry to wake you—'

'Dear God, Anna. What is it?' His eyes are heavy with sleep.

I step inside the dark room, my hands stinging from pounding on the door.

'Uncle, you must do something.' My voice is breathless. 'He is here for Grip. To kill Grip.'

Uncle has lit a candle. He wears brown pyjamas, and a blanket cast hurriedly across his shoulders. He looks so old, so tired.

'Anna. Anna. What are you talking about?'

'The prisoner. Hess.'

His eyes are open now. He shakes his head. 'Anna. There is no prisoner here—'

'I saw him! I stood not five feet from him.'

'You are to stay away from King's House. Do you understand?'

Uncle looks at me with pleading eyes.

'He was at the roost. I don't know why – why the guards weren't watching him. I went to check – Grip was calling – and he was *there*. He means to kill Grip, Uncle. That is *why* he is here. Don't you see? He is here on purpose. Oakes let him in. Now he knows the prophecy – he knows about the Tower ravens.'

'Anna, there is no—'

'Stop lying to me.'

'Anna,' he begins again, but my voice rises over his.

'Stop lying. Stop. Please.'

'My dear, this prisoner is top secret. No one knows he is here. No one. Yeoman Oakes did not let him in – Hess was captured, in a field in Scotland. He is under guard – the best guard in the world. Do not fear him. Grip is safe, and so are you. Now go to bed, please.'

I go. My body is heavy with exhaustion; my mind spins. To have been *that* close to such an evil man, to a Nazi.

What would Timothy Squire say to that? How brave I was. Flo will never believe it, not a word of it.

With a start, I remember the note Hess handed to me.

We are allowed fires again, and the flames bring welcome heat to the damp room. I reach into my coat, take out the small paper. It is a poem. I cannot keep it, not something given to me by a German. *Not even to show Flo the proof.*

I read it once, mouthing the words, before adding it to the flames.

LET THE WAVES IN THUNDER ROAR,
LIFE OR DEATH MAY BE YOUR LOT —
WHETHER WRECKED OR SAFE TO SHORE,
EVER STAY YOUR OWN PILOT.

Tuesday, 27 May 1941

The smiling face of Hess dissolves. No guards stand outside the King's House. On the Green, too, the Warders have left, and the watchfulness of the Tower seems at rest. Grip is fine, if somewhat flustered by the late-night visitor.

I hurry back to the Bloody Tower in hopes of an early breakfast. If Uncle is in the Stone Kitchen alone, maybe I can ask him more about what happened to Hess. Why was he here? Did he really fly to Britain to make peace with Churchill? *But Uncle will never tell me.*

But Uncle is not alone. I can tell before I reach the door. He is talking to Oakes. Just hearing his voice, I can see his bald spot even through the stone wall. Why is he at breakfast so early? At first I think they are discussing Hess; they are not. They are talking about me. *Is that all they do? Hide behind closed doors and talk about me?*

'What she did, yes, it is tragic, but it is also pure selfishness.'

Me? *Is* Uncle cross with me?

'Please, Henry. Her husband – the girl's father, after the war broke out... She needed to protect her. At any cost.'

Uncle cuts him off. 'It was a senseless, twisted scheme. The child should have been evacuated. With her school or with some group. Overseas, the countryside, wherever they would take her. She should not be here. It is not safe. Anna does not belong here.'

I don't hear anything after that.

I do not belong here.

So I will leave. All day I have planned it. But first there is something I must do.

I try to lure Grip back to his cage. The sick bird does not meet my gaze, but waddles silently into the roost. I place the meagre food beside him, closer than I would normally dare, before taking a slow step back. Grip glances at the meat, and finally at me. Does he know? Know that I am keeping a shred with me? I need to.

You understand.

Whether the bird understands or not, he turns to his food, eating weakly. He is half his usual size, and clearly very ill. No croaking, not a single *Orrk*. There is something deeply unsettling about a silent bird. Uncle would diagnose an infection. I know better.

I close the cage tightly.

I cannot wait. By the morning feeding, they will notice that Raven Grip is dying. The last of the Tower ravens. Hope will be lost. *If the ravens leave the Tower, the kingdom will fall.* I remember the prime minister's words, hear the serious, gravel voice in my head.

Hitler's eagles are no match for Britain's ravens.

The words ring around my thoughts.

She should not be here. Wherever they would take her.

I may not belong here, but Mabel does.

I kneel down, speaking through the bars.

'Grip, don't be scared. Oakes is mean, but he will not hurt you. If Mr Brodie returns, it is okay. He is not a terrible man, not truly. Uncle will keep you safe. You are more important to him than anything else.'

My voice cracks on the last words.

I stand, take a long breath. I move from foot to foot. Ravens respond better to motion than stillness. I ensure that he sees, truly *sees* me. I watch Grip for another minute before I speak.

'Don't worry. I will bring her back.'

No one escapes the Tower alone.

I have help, even if he doesn't know it.

Entering the barracks is easy. Even from here shouts of laughter ring out from the tavern; voices singing 'Roll Out the Barrel'. No one is inside.

I take the steps slowly, feeling with my toes for each one, my hand on the curving wall. Blind, I go on, twisting into darkness, the whole left side of my body leaning against the stone. I am not frightened, not this time.

Finally, the stairs come to an end; the floor is level. I am here.

Timothy Squire's flat.

I take the nail from my pocket. *Getting through a locked door is nothing.* Sliding the nail into the keyhole, I try to remember his exact instructions.

Just sweep it around until you feel the catch, then twist – and push.

It takes a minute, and makes a little more noise than I hoped, but I *do* feel the catch. I twist, hard, and lean my shoulder against the door.

It pushes open.

I take a step into the room. My breathing relaxes as I close the door softy behind me. I am alone.

Of course Timothy Squire has left most of his stuff behind. I am looking for something in particular. Something even he would not bring along with him to the countryside.

You stole from my room, remember? It's only fair.

Once I am inside his room I risk using the torch I bought when Nell took me to Boots. Rummaging through the closet – *so many comic books* – I finally find it, wrap it tightly in my jumper and hold it inside my coat. It is small, but heavy.

I feel for a moment the great heat, the searing pain of that night I saved Malcolm. Instinctively, my hand reaches for my hair.

It is nothing anymore, only an empty piece of metal. Only a trick.

It's a dud, he said.

Oh, Timothy Squire, please tell me you weren't lying about this.

I put the thought from my mind, focusing instead on negotiating the narrow steps downwards. I make it back with only one missed step and a muffled curse. I still don't risk the torch, and push quietly through the door and hurry across the Green.

Warders pace before the watch post. I come to a stop in front of the White Tower.

I wait, watching the barracks clock: 9.49 p.m. The Ceremony of the Keys is about to begin. A Warder in a red coat emerges from the Byward Tower, a lantern in his hand. The elaborate ritual of locking the Tower is under way. Once Uncle told me the ceremony had never been interrupted in 700 years.

That is about to end.

I'm sorry, Uncle. But you're right. *I don't belong here.*

I slip the silver metal free, place it gently on the ground, in plain sight, directly in his path to Traitors' Gate. Less than one minute. *Oh, Timothy Squire, you horrible boy, you promised this was safe.*

Swiftly, I turn the corner and hurry towards the West Gate.

I have warm clothes and an extra jumper – the heaviest I could find. Mrs Ballard's hat I have left behind in my room. If anyone sees me, they will think me a boy.

Uncle lied to me. He lied to me about what really happened to Mum; he lied about wanting me to be here at all. Horrible Oakes, talking about Mum – about me! I see them all, Oakes and Miss Breedon and Timothy Squire, laughing, lying, stealing. And even Mr Brodie, driven mad enough to kill poor MacDonald. *I must be free from this place.* And then, almost at the same moment, *I must save them all.*

Just as I expected, a deep voice cries into the night.

'Shelter! Move, everyone to the shelter! Incendiary!'

A whistle screeches through the darkness, soon echoed from the north.

Certain everyone is headed to the shelter, I begin to run back across the parade grounds. Panting, I reach the Casemates, up the steps to the crown of Brass Mount. The flint-towered walls sprawl down to the cold Thames.

There. A drainpipe. Timothy Squire may have been teasing me, but it is my only chance. If I can climb down the drainpipe and drop into the rubbish dump in the moat, I'll be in the Tower Hill gardens.

Voices shout for order, more in confusion than fear. *I*

have little time. They will see that is not a raid, just an old empty bomb.

Problems immediately arise. From the moment I press the thin metal between my fingers, I know the drainpipe will never hold. As soon as it takes my weight, it will snap, crashing down a hundred feet into the darkness.

There is no time. I *must* leave.

I hurriedly throw a leg over the side. It is not too far. My other leg is over, hands alone holding me up. My right foot finds a space between the stones, my left another. I climb down the wall.

Twisting, I release my left hand from the jagged stone, and with desperate fingers grab the next hold. I draw my eyes up from the invisible ground below, look straight ahead. My mouth has gone completely dry.

If only if I can reach the next hold, I might be able to—

Too quickly, I realize, and my foot slips on the next hold. I drop hard on to the grass below.

Balk.

For a moment I am unsure what has happened, my breath crushed out of me.

Balk.

The noise. It is a hen, cackling from its perch. I have lost my jumper and, I realize immediately after, my knife.

I scramble around in the dark allotment and see, among the tall shoots (carrots?), the glint of metal. My jumper too is tangled among the rough leaves. The tiny silver dog is safe in my pocket.

I stand, my eyes drawn to the gleaming river. I look south, where the city of London hides in the safety of darkness. For a brief moment I imagine if the moat still held water – filthy, stinking water filled with bodies – and quickly begin to climb the steep slope. The hens have been shut up for the night; I do not even think about the pigs. I am back on my feet, my legs moving on their own.

A gull calls shrilly from above. Keeping left, I pass the permanent scaffold and gallows, leap over the low wall, pass All Hallows Church, and hurry towards Great Tower Street. *I have done it.*

The summer night air comes cool and crisp. Again, I have forgotten the gloves. I stand tall, looking back. The wind blows endlessly along the river.

I stare hard at the Tower, the old turrets and battlements. I think of the Warders, not just Uncle, but all those who protected me and gave me a home. I must do this, for all of them.

My eyes are drawn to a flash of light on the east wall. A torch.

I freeze in terror. Did the Watchman hear me sneaking away? I squint into the darkness of the bridge and see the steady cone of light. My stomach rises.

A Warder, peering over the edge. The light is on me.

Somehow, even in the black night, I know the face. Oakes. From the great distance we stare at each other. *He recognizes me.*

I should say something, yell back some curse, throw up my hands in confusion, in anger. Instead I turn towards the city and run.

VI

THE RAVENMASTER

We two alone will sing like birds i' the cage.

King Lear, V.iii.9

14

Tuesday, 27 May 1941

Along Great Tower Street, and crossing two broad roads, I run, so fast that even Flo would never catch me. St Paul's, swathed in darkness, I can barely make out. I keep running, along narrow alleys and lanes glittering in a snowfall of powdered glass. Everywhere I look, empty window sockets, melted pipes, sandbagged doorways. Moonlight jumps through the buildings.

Without the street signs, it is impossible to orientate myself. Must they take down *all* the signs? The dust here is different than in the Tower, heavy yellow clouds. The largest city in the world, and my only guide is the occasional tree, ringed with three white bands of paint. *And the smell is like the Underground.*

Oakes will send out Warders. Or will he simply set guards to ensure that I don't return? *You put an incendiary in the middle of the Tower.* He will have you arrested if you return.

There is no sense dwelling on it. I have no choice.

When I see Mabel, I will wrap her inside the jumper and hold her still inside my coat. I clear my head of any thoughts of her great beak and sharp talons.

I must find her, and bring her home.

I stare into the night until my eyes burn. All around, piles of ruins. Are people... buried in there? Did the houses fall in on them? The huge masses of crushing stone, the downed telephone poles. The raid was so long ago. Surely repairs have at least *started*.

This is not a high street, that much I can tell. The front of one house has been sheared off. Is there someone in there? I see a table, leaning at a bizarre angle; glass and bricks everywhere. With horror I notice a shape moving in the shattered building. Before I can cry out, the shape leaps suddenly forward and races past, a clock in his hands.

Looters, I realize in disgust. *Of course it's not him. Where? Where are you going?*

I will need to wait for dawn, when Mabel wakes. *And then what?*

The voice is cancelled by a distant light, faint blue and high above. At any moment, the siren will wail. *Why isn't it wailing?*

'Hey! You there!'

The voice is loud. Without thinking, I am off and gal-loping. A patrolling warden. What does he want? To arrest me? I dodge the debris, my feet oddly heavy. Panic makes it impossible to focus. The warden is probably yelling at the looter. Likely he didn't even see me.

A quick glance over my shoulder shows that he is chasing me.

Move.

My sense of direction is confused. Have I turned east again?

After several endless minutes I huddle against the bricks, panting quietly. I slow down my thoughts; breathe. Why is he hunting me when a raid is about to start? *Is this a raid? Where is the siren?*

What did Timothy Squire say again? His voice comes to me, I can hear it clearly; all it says, over and over, is *run*. I run.

Faint cries from the darkness. I need a shelter. There is meant to be a distance of only eight minutes between them. I am running and I see nothing. Not a Tube station, railway arch, or even a doorway. No *Public Shelter* sign.

I will have to find my own. Lifting my feet, again and again, trying not to fall. There. Across the street, a white concrete building, a red flag on the roof. I push the heavy door. It is not locked.

For a moment I stand in the new darkness, my eyes slowly adjusting. Outside, any moment now, will come the whistle and crunch of bombs. Will this concrete protect

me? I don't know, but it has to be safer than the streets.
The warden too will have to make for cover.

But the siren never came.

I slide down the wall and keep near the entrance,
remembering to stay near the doorway. I clutch the silver
dog in my pocket. Outside sounds fall silent.

Nothing happens.

As my eyes take ages to adapt, a smell settles, heavy
and powerful. A familiar smell, something I remember
from home. It is very strong, and I wonder how I didn't
notice it immediately.

I will survive at least until I find Mabel.

Another sound, close. Guns restarting? I inch nearer
to the doorway. Why has nobody else taken shelter here?
Unless they have, and dozens of strange men and women
sit crowded in the corners. Somehow I am sure that I am
alone, here in the darkness with the pungent smell. Like
Flo's father's car. Why is the siren still silent?

I take a moment to check my things. I have food, in
addition to Mabel's food, but only a bite. How am I
expecting to find a black bird in the vast city? At least,
I am sure, she is not in here, under a concrete roof and
surrounded by…

My heart does not beat. I cannot move. Yet I must, and
now. I know where I am, why I am the only one sheltering
here. The heavy smell.

I know now what this building is.

A fuel depot.

Day is slow to arrive. I walk the quiet streets. No siren wails; no bombs fall. I am merely tired, exhausted, seeing and hearing things in this broken city. Dawn is only a few minutes away. The outlines of buildings are almost clear.

A whole night, hiding from an imaginary raid. *In a fuel depot.* Timothy Squire will never hear a word of this. Even Flo would laugh at me.

Serves me right for what I did with the bomb at the Tower.

What would the warden have said if he caught me sneaking out of there, thinking it was a shelter? *Lock me in a mad house?*

'Hey!'

It seems I am about to find out. It is the bloody warden again, and I am running, directly towards an entrance like a cave in the mountains. Someone is standing in a doorway, a woman, and she pulls me inside.

Valerie has invited me to sit and have tea, 'Blitz soup' and toast. She is the owner of The Rose and Punchbowl and she has even dealt with the nosy warden. When I ask if I can please use the lavatory, she points to the back.

The mirror shows a small, pale face, lost and frightened, with ragged hair like a boy's. I don't know where I am, where Raven Mabel is, how to get home, *if* I can even go home… The smell of toasting bread pulls me back.

I return to the table, trying to smile. My legs, heavy and sore, are grateful for the rest. And the fire, roaring in the grate.

She sees my look, gestures to the plate. I begin to eat. Mum used to go lunching with a woman named Valerie – Valerie Willis – and I never liked the look of her. This Valerie, however, with her short black curls and firm jaw, seems kind. For some reason she reminds me of Nell. A kindly Nell.

As she watches me, Valerie asks questions, quiet and unhurried, ducking her head whenever she speaks.

'What about you, dear? You live in the Tower, you said. That must be quite something.'

I nod, and return to the toasted bread. It is warm and delicious.

'Hmm. I always thought of that place as some kind of tomb. But I suppose the whole city is, nowadays. Living in that old medieval castle, though. You always walk around by yourself at night?'

'Yes. I mean, I have to be back by sunrise – I'm the Ravenmaster now – so I need to be back for the dawn feeding.'

'Aha. Well, just enjoy your toast for now. Worry about the birds later.'

She does not believe me – it *does* sound strange, and with my hair I must look a right mess – but I don't try to explain further. It doesn't matter. I have toast and tea and a kind woman to talk to. I shift towards the warm and welcome fire. I think of Nell, trying to frame my questions politely.

'So you work here?' I ask.

'You're in my pub, dear. Bought it just before the war started. Not the best bit of luck. Beats getting torched by a bomb, though.'

I think of all the damage along the street and though I don't say anything, it seems Valerie can see my thoughts easily enough.

'Last raid, bomb fell right outside.' She tosses her head dismissively. 'Can't even explode properly. I watched it just simpering away.'

'You didn't go down to the shelter?'

'No one bothers any more. Only the crazies in there now. *I'm ill, I'm ill*, is all they say.'

She is eyeing me strangely. She thinks I'm one of the crazies. A thirteen-year-old, the Ravenmaster at the Tower of London, wandering the East London streets at night? Hollow laughter builds up inside me.

I try to block out my time cowering in a fuel depot because of an imagined siren. I turn back to what's left of the soup, eating noisily but unable to slow down.

'Thank you so much,' I say, my spoon scraping against the porcelain bowl. 'I was terribly hungry.'

'You can't count on the food centres. Have you *seen* the queues outside the Exchange? Even during a raid nobody moves. The staff shut it up and run for cover, but not a person budges out of that line. We have to rely on each other.'

I smile up at her. Even with the generous meal, the ache in my stomach won't fade. 'I heard Prime Minister Churchill's speech. He said – he said the people of the East End have been the most brave during the war.'

'Suits him fine, doesn't it? "Hey look, the Cockneys aren't grumbling. And who's not better than a Cockney?" Yeah, some people around here are putting up with an awful lot. But we were just as brave when there was no work, when we got sick, when food ran out. It's not a compliment to say it now, just 'cause bombs are falling. Nobody asks for his applause.'

I sit in silence, unsure what I can possible say. Surely it *is* a compliment, that they keep on working when people are dying all around? And what is so wrong with applause, whether you ask for it or not? The look on Valerie's face says otherwise. I remember that Mum used to say 'No one's brave. People just have different ways of looking at the world.'

Little else is spoken on any topic. Valerie only says that I should stay and warm up until day breaks, and then begins her own day of setting up the pub. Dawn is not yet here. And I can use a few moments' rest by the fire.

Pots bang in the back room. The chair is warm, comfortable. Different from the ones at the Tower, I flip through the black headlines of the newspapers. *Berlin Claims 1,000 Tonnes of Bombs on London.*

The *Evening Standard* is in the pile. I have not seen a single copy, not even among the stacks in the Casemates shelter. Mum didn't like me reading it either; she didn't *hide* it from me.

I recognize the strange, difficult-to-read font of the paper's title. The headlines, grave though they are, seem warm, familiar: *Bismarck Sunk. Ulster Not To Have Conscription.*

I flip the thin pages, remembering the lettering, the sections. It looks almost the same. Eight pages. One penny. I turn to the back, before *Amusements* and *Radio.* Her writing would be right here, usually, though sometimes it was closer to the front. And then I see an article I somehow missed. An excerpt from a German paper, translated.

> *The Party authorities state: Party leader Hess, who had been expressly forbidden by the Fuhrer to use an aeroplane because of a disease which had been becoming worse for years, was, in contradiction of this order, able to get hold of a plane.*
>
> *His family have been cleared of any involvement. His*

wife, Frau Ilse Prohl, has sued for divorce on the grounds of desertion and insanity.

'*Evening Standard*. Used to read that one myself,' comes a voice. Valerie, wiping the bar, is still watching me. 'Now it's full of the same lies as the others.'

I nod knowingly. My eyes turn back to the little ads. *Nicholson's Gin. It's Clear – It's Good.*

'Damn shame they lost her. Someone actually talking about the war.' She keeps wiping, talking almost to herself.

For some reason, I refuse to look up, staring hard at the ads. *Lifebuoy Soap. Olive Oil Brushless Shave.* It doesn't stop her voice.

'Imagine, with all the people dying like they are – in bombs and fire and crushed in the shelters. Imagine, ending it like that?'

I blink rapidly. I don't know who she is talking about – she could be talking about anyone – but my heart surges. Ending it like *what*?

She is talking about someone else – the *Evening Standard* must have so many different woman journalists. Mum was against the war, but she was definitely not alone. *Ending it like what?*

Uncle's voice comes back to me, unbidden.

A terrible, tragic mistake.

I say goodbye to Valerie, assuring her I know the way. She makes me leave with a bun wrapped in newspaper – the *Manchester Guardian* – and I exit the pub.

It makes me so angry, that they all knew. Uncle and Oakes and Timothy Squire. That Valerie from East London knew. That everyone knew about Mum except me.

You knew. You always knew.

A wretched old woman stares from her door as I pass. Behind her, the house is blown open. There is a cloth on the table, pictures on the wall. A short staircase climbs to a floor that is no longer there. Some yellow flowers grow in their pot. Across the street, not ten feet away, a busted hydrant shoots a fountain of water high into the air. *You always knew.*

A family – a large family – carrying packs and clothes, trudges past. I stand, still, watching them step over the debris, broken wood and collapsed stone. They seem to go on forever, a line of dirty, unsmiling women and men.

'God bless you, dear.'

It is the old woman from the doorway. She gestures to the filthy line of people marching on.

'Are you with them?'

I shake my head. 'What are they doing?'

'Trekking.'

'Trekking.' I repeat the unfamiliar word. 'Going where?'

'This lot? Epping Forest, I gather. I'll find out soon enough myself.'

A pause.

'You have somewhere to live, little girl?'

I am *not* a little girl. But my head is shaking and the word escapes me. 'No.'

'Bomb?'

I nod.

'Not from around here, though, eh? No matter, no matter. Hitler will make us all neighbours before long.'

I smile back. 'Are *you* going... to Epping Forest?'

Wrinkled eyes stare into the distance. 'It's safer there. I've nowhere else to go.'

I reach into my coat, take out the tightly wrapped bun. 'Here.'

For a moment she stares down at the bundle, the smell of it in the air. Then she looks up at me.

'No, dear. No, that is rightly yours, however you came by it. Keep it until your belly rumbles again. If you're off with this lot, that won't be too long. It's a mighty walk up to the forest.'

I think about it. *We are not ourselves in this. We all do what we must.* Then I see another image: a large inquisitive face, liquid black eyes.

With a strange feeling, a *crumbling* inside, I know the truth. Mum was wrong about no one being brave, about people just having different ways of looking at the world. It is having to be brave that makes you brave.

We all do what we must.

'Here,' I say, again offering the bun. 'I have just eaten, more than my fill, on account of a helpful stranger. Please take this.'

Her head shakes but her eyes never leave the bun.

'If you will not take it, can you carry it with you?' I push it into her suddenly greedy hands. 'For one of the others – a child, perhaps.'

The bun has disappeared into the layers of her coats. 'A fine thing to do. A kind one, you are.'

For a moment we stand, silent in the rising light. I wish the old woman good luck.

As I reach the corner, I turn. The old woman has not moved to follow the trekkers. She stands, stock still, and even from the distance I can see her mouth furiously working.

The sun has risen over the buildings. *Where am I going?* I have wandered far. Many roads and bridges are closed, and I'm lost.

Where is he? No, he is out in the country somewhere. I am *not* searching for him. All the thoughts I've had – guessing at which northern town he could be in, whether or not it had a port so I could convince him to come to Montreal with me – all of that is silenced.

I must find Raven Mabel. That is why I am here.

I try Uncle's 'secret whistle', but nothing happens. It doesn't matter. I will find her somehow.

Then, as if waiting for my resolve, there she is. On a distant wire, tall and proud, with piled black feathers. Raven Mabel. I cannot believe my luck. How is it possible? *No time.* Casually the bird takes wing, miraculous, becoming lighter than air. I race after her.

Mabel veers east, a dark spot on the grey sky, and after a few seconds I can no longer distinguish the bird from the mist. She is gone. No, she is there, doubling back to land on a ledge. And she is off again.

Faces and landmarks blur past. Yet I see nothing except the streak of black above, coasting, disappearing behind the clouds, long wings confidently riding the wind. From time to time the bird perches on a lamp post or gutter, waiting for me to catch up, before flying grimly on.

The bird is leading me. How is it possible?

She has landed again. Now she does not fly on. Above, the Queen's Head sign creaks in the wind. I am close. I take another cautious step. The words lunge in my mind, jump at me, and I try to avoid them.

It isn't her. It was never her.

I come closer, carefully taking the bloody piece of meat from my pocket. I give Uncle's secret whistle, and this time it sounds clear and strong in the still air.

It isn't her.

'Good morning, Raven Mabel,' I call softly. 'This is for you. It is from Raven Grip. He wants you to come home.'

Caw. Caw.

'He is lonely there – and sick, too. Come on, we have to go and see him. He needs us, you see. We have to be there for him.'

I place the slimy meat gently along the brick ledge, near several empty pint glasses, and step back as I always do. The bird turns, takes a tentative step forward.

I try the whistle again, louder this time. Mabel just watches me. She is hungry, starving. That is why she looks so small, so much like a common crow. It is *her*. It is her and I will bring her back to the Tower and Raven Grip will live, and Uncle will smile, and everyone will have hope again.

It is not her. It is not even a raven. A common crow, nothing more.

The bird skulks across the ledge, oily black wings trailing behind her, claws clicking on the brick. After a brief inspection of me, the bird reaches the meat, pecks at it.

What happens next is a blur. All at once, I feel it zoning in. A quick upward glance reveals a dark mass, falling heavily, plunging towards me.

Two birds now perch on the ledge. A harried crow, its faint outline walking away, and, eating the meat, staring proudly down at me, a giant raven.

I walk along Great Tower Street, Mabel strangely quiet and content inside my coat. I wrapped her in my jumper just as I've seen Uncle wrap her in a towel to carry her inside for the animal doctor. She barely resisted.

She must have heard the whistle. I can't believe it. *Even Timothy Squire couldn't make up a story like this.*

Yeoman Oakes can try and stop me. At least Uncle will let me return her to her cage. If Uncle wants me to leave, he will have to tell me himself. I will tell him I know the truth about Mum. I will tell him he doesn't need to lie any more. Then I will leave.

Where will I go? Tilbury Docks? Epping Forest? No, I will go back to my house in Warwick Avenue. *Home.* Whatever is left of it.

Mabel is heavy. But she is quiet and still, and when I glance down to ensure she is OK, the great liquid eyes meet my own. Raven Grip, at least, will not hate me.

The sun is rising. I cross the cobblestones and step on to the bridge.

I have brought Mabel back to the Tower.

The guard sees me approach. His blue coat is bright in the growing sunlight.

I have no excuse this time, no bribe of fish, no Timothy Squire and his cheeky grin. If Oakes wants me arrested, there is nothing I can do. *Once he pulled me from a fire. Now he's pushing me back in.*

I remember that the Watchman's name is Mr Thorne. I take a deep breath. I don't even have my ID card. I can only pray that he is in a good mood.

Or am I imagining things? I have not slept in over a day. By the time I reach the archway, there is no one in the box. That is queer. No guard? Or has something just happened – something terrible that drew him away? I enter the Tower in silence.

As I walk up towards the Green, everything looks as it always is. Warders on duty, Wives clacking across the stone. Did the Watchman leave his post just as I came up the bridge? Or was he expecting me? Did he let me pass unquestioned?

I decide to head straight for the cages, my strides normal and purposeful. Already I can see that Uncle has not yet opened them for the dawn feeding. Has nobody noticed that I was gone? Is it possible?

A smile overpowers me as I swing open the cage. I take Mabel from my coat, set her gently down. My jumper is stained, powdery and whitish, and the smell both sick and sweet. I don't care. The two birds observe one another in

silence. Then high, knocking sounds erupt. *Toc-toc-toc.*
Toc-toc-toc. It is a cheerful sound, a welcoming, both
harsh and lovely, and I feel suddenly as if I am intruding
on a private celebration.

'You're up early.'

I freeze. But a strength of will comes to me, and I turn
to face him.

'Good morning, Yeoman Oakes.' My voice wavers
slightly. I catch it. 'Raven Mabel has returned.'

'So I can see. This is excellent news.'

He is smiling; something about the smile tells me that I
don't understand what is happening.

'Your uncle will be thrilled.'

I stare at him in silence.

'It has been a most unusual night – a trying night.' He
exhales loudly. 'For both of us, perhaps.'

Exhaustion breaks over me like a wave. *Punish me how
you like.* Arrest me. Add my name to your stupid book on
the prisoners of the Tower. It doesn't matter now.

'Anna, you may think me an odd man, but I do have
a special concern for you.' The smile is gone. 'You see, I
myself have not been feeling terribly well. Already I can
recognize the symptoms in you. Even in this early light...
yes, you seem quite pale.'

I can say nothing, the weight of exhaustion pulling me
to the ground.

'In fact, I must recommend that you go straight to bed,
and remain there until you are feeling quite better.' The

smile has returned. 'But, first, there is someone here to see you.'

I must look dumbfounded, as if a bomb hit me and didn't explode. Oakes clears his throat softly and leads me on. Why hasn't he sent me away? Why is he being nice to me, a girl with no parents who docsn't belong anywhere.

I walk the steps, unsure. A man in a tweed blazer and hat stands at the West Gate. He leans on an umbrella. For a second I am reminded of Churchill, that first day he came to visit. This man is tall, and much thinner than the Prime Minister. As I step closer I realize it is not a man at all; it is a boy. In his time away he appears to have grown, his cheeks ruddy from the country.

My smile is huge and wide and probably terrifying.

'Timothy Squire.'

He has no chance to speak; I have folded him into a hug big enough to break his thin bones. When did he return? Did he know somehow that I have been searching for him across the city, worrying when the bombs fell north?

After a moment he looks down, serious, then he pulls me close again. His lips are soft. Even though he presses too hard, I don't pull away.

I whip round, flustered and red, but Oakes has found another wall to captivate him.

'Well,' Timothy Squire says finally, turning clumsily away. He squints at my face, my hair. 'You look different. Something… is different. I mean, you look nice, Anna.'

'Thank you, Timothy Squire.'

He gives a shallow cough. 'So my parents are going to bloody furious. But I figured Grip must be getting a bit lonely. Thought you might need some help chopping the meat.'

'I need your help, do I?'

He squirms a bit, flashes a smile. 'What d'you reckon? I have to send a letter to Mum and Dad straightaway, telling them I've come back. But first we can stop and see Grip. If you'd like.'

He has removed his cap, and his hair is almost as long as mine. Dark and bushy as ever, and his forehead just as large.

'I suppose I could use an assistant,' I say. 'You'll do.'

Even as we start walking, he is speaking.

15

Mabel and Grip are moulting, their beautiful feathers unkempt and turning copper at the edges (Grip's turn almost brown), before falling off in heaps of feathers around the roost. Mabel is the more dramatic moulter, her pink head visible through her sudden baldness.

'Don't worry, Mabel,' I say in sympathy. 'New feathers always grow back.'

The birds don't handle it well, pottering over the cobblestones with resentment. It is several weeks of indignity. My hair has grown faster than I thought. Another couple weeks and I'll have a bob again. Mabel will be fine.

Not all old feathers fade, and when I find a perfectly preserved one, glossy and ink-black, I put it in my pocket. I'm not certain if it's Mabel's or Grip's but I will add it to my diary. It says more than any words can.

Timothy Squire's parents may have been bloody

furious, but they did return. And the whole family seems happy enough to be back.

Uncle's health has improved sufficiently to resume his dusk-feeding duties, and his smile is wide as he sees Mabel and Grip together. I watch them too. Already new bumps along her rounded skull mark coming feathers.

'A little miracle,' he says. 'I had thought her as good as lost.'

'Me too. It was your whistle, Uncle Henry. She heard it and came home.'

That part at least is true. *Just not from where you think.*

'Surely a good sign. A sign of hope.'

I agree, and together we go to dinner. Oakes shows no sign of giving up my secret.

After dinner – pork has even returned to the table – Uncle and I sit alone. I am happy, feeling almost light, but Uncle's words from that night on the staircase still linger.

I look at him, at my uncle, his soft eyes.

'Can you tell me what happened to Mum?'

'Your mother was killed, my dear.'

I pause. 'Not by a bomb, though.'

'She was killed by this war, Anna. She was a strong woman – but this war…'

I am aware of his gaze, flitting over the room, never once looking at me. I remember too how Oakes is always talking about the gas mask, yet never quite able to look at it.

'She hated the war, Anna. She loved you – so much…'
He sighs, a great, pained sound. 'I received a letter from
your mum just before she died. It said very little. We
hadn't spoken in many years. The letter only said that she
wanted me to take care of you. That you would be safer
here, with me.'

'You didn't believe it?' I say into the silence.

'Wanting you to come and live with me and Gregory?'
He shakes his head. 'Nothing could be harder to believe.'

'What did she want to protect me from?'

'The war. These walls are strong.'

'She didn't need to die for me to come here.'

'No.' For a long moment he is quiet. He removes his
glasses, wipes an eye with the back of his hand, and
perches them again on his nose. 'She made a great mistake,
Anna. She loved you.'

'But the bus…?'

'The headmaster thought it was best. I'm afraid I agreed
with him.'

I nod. There is nothing else to say. He is telling the
truth, I know. Not all of it, I think, but it is enough. The
business of adults.

She loved you. She hated this war. She made a terrible,
tragic mistake. She needed to protect you. At any cost.

She loved you.

It is enough.

Thursday, 14 August 1941

I smile into the bright wind. From the ramparts the vast world opens up before me. I feel light-headed, unsteady on my feet. But smiling. Speechless and smiling. The summer dress that Nell helped me pick, a simple pattern of red flowers, is loose. My hair is once again in a bob. My feet are *bare*.

Timothy Squire and I walk across the Green, through the deep shadows and waves of drenching sun. Mabel and Grip shuffle close by.

And then, crashing into the newly painted world, comes Oakes.

'Anna,' he says. 'Timothy. A beautiful day.'

'It is, sir,' I say.

'The ravens seem happy, don't they?'

I nod warily. He hasn't got to his point yet. He looks down at us, smiles.

I see an image of Oakes, staring across the ramparts as I escaped into the night. *He didn't tell Uncle.* Maybe not, but what does he want?

'Well, Anna, I was wondering, if you are interested, whether you two cared to join me at the cathedral?'

'At St Paul's?'

Oakes nods. 'You're supposed to be over forty to join the Watch, but I think it will be all right just for one evening. I'll tell them you're my secretaries.'

'Secretary?' says Timothy Squire.

Oakes sees his frown, does not apologize. 'Etymologically, a secretary is the person you trust with your secrets.'

Timothy Squire nods, still uncertain. I almost smile.

'What do you think? There hasn't been a raid in a while, but we need to be ready. I thought, as you're not able to leave the Tower very often, it might be nice for you.' Although he is smiling, it doesn't seem like a trap. If anything, I feel a rush of affection for Oakes.

'Give it some thought,' he says. 'If you want to come, meet me tomorrow night at the West Gate.' He turns back before he leaves. 'You're not afraid of heights, are you? No? Good. Tomorrow night then.'

I hadn't noticed as I dashed through the city, but the cathedral is more visible than ever. The buildings around it have been razed and now it looks massive and exposed.

I am a member of the St Paul's Night Watch. There are around forty others, I am told, but only a dozen come each night. All in blue overalls, webbed belts and steel helmets, gathered round the choir stalls. They don't look so silly when they're all together.

'This is Anna Cooper,' Oakes says, introducing me. 'She looks after the ravens at the Tower. And Timothy Squire, who gives her a hand.'

I feel another surge of affection for Oakes that I can tell Timothy Squire does not share.

All of the members are men, about the age of the Warders (so they wouldn't be called up), though many are shorter, slighter. Mostly they are architects, I discover, or lovers of buildings. One is a historian. Each one knows the cathedral as well as Uncle knows the Tower.

Light pours into the great chamber, until the sun, smouldering, disappears.

There is no raid, so we go down to the crypt and drink tea, talking while two men play chess on a camp bed.

I learn much about the cathedral. There are twenty staircases. It is dark, as dark as the Tower in places. Twenty-eight bombs hit St Paul's in the 29 December raid. I hear about the Watch's amazing training. How members are taken to a remote corner of the huge building, and then tasked to find their way back, alone in the darkness. Then certain passages are said to be unusable – pretend debris has clogged it, or a bomb has struck there – and each test gets harder. *Far better than our school examinations.*

Oakes, it turns out, is part of the 'dome patrol'. He has, at times, crawled along the wooden beams high above the nave, once in order to extinguish an incendiary that threatened the organ.

'I remember when Henry first brought you into the Tower. The look on your face.'

'Like a terrified child.'

'Like a regular girl. Maybe a little tired,' he adds with a smile. 'But after... everything... to be so normal. *That* is remarkable.'

'Extraordinary,' I correct him gently.

Whatever Oakes thinks of Churchill, he laughs now to hear me repeat his joke.

Timothy Squire is invited to play a game, and he picks up the chess pieces with enthusiasm. *Boys and their games.* I have a sudden thought.

'I am sorry,' I say, 'about Wembley. I know Uncle wanted to go with you.'

Oakes shakes his head; there is a strange look in his eyes. 'Me? Oh no. I'm barely a Preston fan, truly.'

'It was pretty boring, sir.'

A smile sweeps back on to his face. 'So I heard. Luckily, it was a one–all draw, so we got to see the rematch a few weeks later. Ewood Park is no Wembley, but the right side won.'

'Yeoman Oakes. I don't want to be awful, but... what is wrong with Uncle? He is sick, isn't he?'

A look, almost of sadness, passes over his face, then is gone. In that moment I don't care who the mysterious German visitor was.

'Yes, he is sick.'

'And it's... quite serious?'

'Yes, your uncle has an illness. And he always will. He has good days and bad ones, like the rest of us. He is a strong man, Anna. Yours is a tough family.'

We stand for a moment in silence.

'Yeoman Oakes, will you teach me more about the carving in Salt Tower some day? I don't know the names of any of the stars.'

He smiles. 'It would be my pleasure, Anna.'

'So?' he says after another quiet minute. 'Do you want to see this view?'

I hear Timothy Squire laughing over some grand play. I look up into the great dome, past the nave and the choir stalls, the high columns and pillars, the gleaming organ pipes and windows, and I smile.

You could see my smile in the dark.

16

I t is time.

Of course, the soldiers are having another dance, and I pass the girls, marching across the cobblestones, laughing in summer dresses. I even see, with a bloom of joy, Nell, in a black chiffon dress and satin shoes, looking as stylish and sophisticated as Mum's friends from the theatre. She is on leave, which suddenly sounds glamorous.

She only has a moment to say hello – she is with the handsome guard, the one who pushed me aside in order to hide Hess – but I will never forget the words she says.

'Good hair, Cooper. Looking snappy.'

'Thank you, Nell. I love your dress.'

From across the Green she winks at me.

My grin soon fades. It is my fault. I spent too long with Timothy Squire. I left Mabel alone, unwatched, unwilling to break up their reunion, even after Uncle warned me. *I thought she'd want to be back.* Already, though, Mabel is gone. *It is all my fault.*

Uncle has taken her second disappearance far worse than her first. He is worried about Grip now. He even secured a bracelet, a circle of heavy yellow plastic, round his foot. 'To identify him,' he said. 'Should he ever get away, he can be found.'

Poor Grip. It is almost as if, as I approach the roost, I can feel his yearning. I shake my head, walk faster. Grip is our last raven and his wings have grown too long. *Always there have been ravens at the Tower of London. Without them the kingdom will fall.*

Timothy Squire said Uncle made up it all up. Made it up to give me hope. To give us all hope.

It is my duty. To Uncle, to all the Warders. To the kingdom. *It is my duty.*

And here he is. He looks up at me through the bars, head tilted, eyes knowing.

'Hello, Grip.'

Shrugging off my bag, I stand before his cage, gloves on, scissors in hand. I pry open the hinge.

He looks at me, his leg stretching in its bracelet. *So he can be found.*

I drop the scissors, pull off the gloves. Grip looks at me as I kneel down and firmly clasp my hand around his wings. He does not move. My other hand reaches in my bag, searching. I find the box, slide it open.

'Goodbye, Grip.'

I hold the knife edge to the bracelet and cut it free.

Uncle looks up. Even though he is getting better, he is still very pale. Good days and bad days, as Oakes said. Like the rest of us.

'It must be time to clip his wings again,' he says.

'Yes,' I answer.

'What is it, my dear?' Uncle struggles to sit up. 'Are you unwell?'

'I am fine, Uncle. It's only that, well, I knew it was time to clip Grip's wings. So I went there now... even though I'd just put him to bed. It was time.'

'Good girl.' He lowers himself slowly down. 'It's our last raven, after all. We must keep a special eye on him.'

'It's just that...' I'm not sure quite what to say. *You've come this far. It's too late now. Go on, you're a bright spark.* 'Uncle, I think I know why Mabel came back. I mean, I'm sure it wasn't for the reason that I thought at first, but for a different reason.'

I am making no sense as words seem to have failed me – nothing that I want to say comes out the way I want it to. Of course, I can't mention my late-night visit to the East End to capture her, but I have to somehow get him to *know*, to understand, what has happened. Whether he is understanding anything is uncertain. He sits quite still, silent, watchful.

'I know it sounds... mad... but I think that Mabel returned because of Grip. And not just because she missed him, which of course she did, but because she wanted to... tell him something.'

What in the world...? It's too late now. *Bright spark, indeed.*

'To tell him about *out there*, about the city and the rooftops and flying. Ravens are very sophisticated birds. What I mean is, I think – I'm *sure* – that she came back to get him. So they could be together, out there.'

Uncle has not moved yet something has changed. He is still watching me, his soft eyes somehow softer, and for a terrifying minute I feel sure that he is going to cry. *Oh, what have I done?*

'Do you know,' he says finally, 'that a group of ravens is called an "unkindness"? But I do not think so.'

'I'm sorry, Uncle. Grip is gone. I just couldn't... I couldn't do it.'

Once again, he moves faster than I could have imagined, and his arms wrap round me and pull me in. I worry about hurting him – he is still so frail – but I can't help squeezing him back. I sit for a long moment, perched on the edge of the small bed, feeling the warmth of Uncle's hug.

Wednesday, 27 August 1941

The late summer sun is shining. I walk beside the Case-mates with Uncle, who seems in fine form. All through breakfast he held court, telling old tales of Grip and Mabel, of the morning Edgar appeared in Chapel, of MacDonald turning the squirrel inside out (*that was MacDonald?*), to the rapt audience of me and Timothy Squire and Oakes.

Yeoman Brodie is back now, too. He winced at the story and apologized again – he seems much better now – and even found time to talk about all the new friends Malcolm has made in the country (I can well imagine), while Yeoman Cecil ate the newly harvested potatoes in quiet satisfaction.

As Uncle and I clamber across the battlements, his new cane ticking on the stone, once again I am the one struggling to keep pace. He must be hot under that buttoned coat. Surely a cloak isn't required *every day*.

'There is talk, any week now, we could open again,' Uncle says, his voice wistful but with a smile in it. 'Can you picture it? People swarming about? Tourists taking photographs?'

I look round at the scorched stones of the White Tower and Salt Tower, the ruins of the Byward Tower, the crumbling buildings of the Main Guard, trying to imagine it, the people, the cameras, the excited children.

'No,' I say.

I am ready, though. Leslie once said that the whole

Tower changes completely – *you can't go anywhere without some bloody West End kid staring. Like living in a bleeding zoo.* But she had smiled, and so do I. Still, it makes me think of her, and the ravens, again.

The loud, calling birds, moving round us, as Timothy Squire and I handed out the biscuits. MacDonald and Cora crowding us, Grip eating in dignified solitude, MacDonald and Cora fighting over the scraps, Edgar and Merlin long finished and looking for more. Laughter amid the croaking birds, the glistening black feathers, the black eyes that *know* you.

I finally got a letter from Flo, forwarded by Headmaster Brownbill, who turns out to know our old form teacher. ('Looks as if your friend likes to write too.') My heart sank when I tore it open – only two lines! – then I read it and laughed so loudly that Sparks gave me a surprised look as he descended into some chamber.

Mother says the bombs are over so we're coming home in November. So tired of Peter and Michael, and Ellen is such a baby. Can I come live with you?

I stared at Flo's words, the letters sloping downhill, my face beaming. This time I let the laughter come crashing out.

Uncle and I come round to the White Tower. Past the scaffold, down towards the empty cages. I take a deep breath.

A crow hobbles past. Uncle raises his cane, points to the great, scarred fortress.

'And they will be here for tomorrow.'

They? I look from Uncle to the cages. He sees my look, smiles brightly.

'But of course, Anna. The new flock will be here by midday. Six adults and a spare. You'll have to help me with the names. We'll give them ID tags too, so others can tell them apart.' He smiles again.

I nod as we walk, clicking towards the empty roost.

'And I think, if you're happy to, you should take over my position as Ravenmaster. Now don't argue – I've earned my rest. Though I'll be free enough to give you a hand, should you need it.'

'Thank you, Uncle.'

'After all, there have always been ravens in the Tower, since the time of Charles II. Without them, my dear, the kingdom would fall.'

'The Crown jewels.'

I squeeze Uncle's hand tightly and we keep walking.

Friday, 26 September 1941

'Hitler's first plan, if we ever surrendered, was to take a pair of mated ravens from the Tower and bring them back with him. You know, to protect Germany.'

I nod as Timothy Squire goes on. Even if he looks

older, he is still the same boy who loves Rockfist Rogan and hunting for bombs and is always curious about everything. Now, it seems, he considers himself an expert on Tower legend and a protector of ravens. The junior Ravenmaster.

Everything feels normal again. The grim towers and turrets, the dark uniforms on the battlements, the coal-black ravens parading round the Green, sunning themselves. *Kraa. Kraa.* Home.

'Seems fair we all got put up to third form,' Timothy Squire says with his grin. 'Brownpants, though? Worse than ever, isn't he? The Blitz ending didn't soften him.'

We climb the east Casemates, now mostly cleaned and repaired. Home to the new school, as well. Timothy Squire sits up front, but every once in a while the giant head will turn and smile at me. *I bet we'll have to make up the summer term.*

'You know the old legend, right?' Timothy Squire says. 'The ravens hold the power of the Crown, so if they fly away, the kingdom will fall. No need to worry, though, they're in good hands.'

Tomorrow is the 27th. The day I lost Mum. A long year has passed. But last night I had a dreamless sleep.

She made a terrible mistake. And I don't need to be reminded that I sacrificed myself, and the fate of the kingdom, for the happiness of a single bird.

She loved you.

I take Timothy Squire's hand in mine. Together we turn

the corner where the new roost, in the soft morning light, shines with a fresh beginning.

I will take him to Warwick Avenue, to see my house, check on the magnolia tree. Perhaps tomorrow we will go.

A commotion sounds at the front gate.

Timothy Squire releases my hand, marches proudly towards the entrance. Ready to show that he is up for it. Mr Thorne the Watchman has stopped a man from entering. A too eager tourist?

Voices grow louder. Timothy Squire turns back, casts me a protective look. *If only you knew.* Whoever the unwanted visitor is, he is not a Nazi leader.

I still cannot see the man, yet his voice reaches me, loud and haggard. A drunken officer, late for a ball?

'Residents only,' the Watchman is saying.

'Let me through.'

I squint, trying to see the figure. I cannot make out the exchange.

'I don't give a damn if he's on death's door,' the voice comes again. There is something – familiar – in the accent, the stern tone. 'Send out Gregory Oakes so I can shoot the bastard myself!'

A horrible chill seizes me. *The German.* It is the same voice as the man from Traitors' Gate. He has come to kill Oakes.

Oakes, oblivious as always, chooses this moment to appear.

'What is it? What is going on here?'

He looks at me and his eyes travel to the fracas at the gate.

'Anna. Get back to your room. Now.'

'No, Mr Oakes, sir – you mustn't.'

But he is racing ahead and I follow. Faster, I slip through the arch before him.

The Watchman has raised his gun, and Timothy Squire stands poised between joining in and running for it. At the sight of the German between them, his hands held up and no weapon drawn, I stop dead.

He is the same – thinner, wilder, but the same man I have glimpsed across the Green. He is not wearing a hat. His hair, thick and ruffled, is pale as moonlight. His ears stick out.

Oakes breaks into the circle.

'Coward,' the German spits. 'She is not in Yorkshire. What right do you have? To hide her from me? Where is she, you snivelling—'

The German, feeling me watching, turns his gaze on me and falls silent. Everyone falls silent. I stand rooted, my mind reeling, flustered by the inconceivable, catching on nothing. Yet certain of the impossible truth.

The German's eyes are locked on mine. There is nothing else in the world.

I don't have to say the word out loud; everyone hears it.

Father.

Acknowledgements

For their generous support, I am indebted to the Arts Council England.

My thanks to Bridget Clifford at the Royal Armouries Museum, Tower of London, for being so generous with her time and knowledge. For championing the idea and helping to bring it into the world, I am extremely grateful to Alex Drago, Megan Gooch, and Ceri Fox at Historic Royal Palaces.

For her wonderful artwork and willingness to tackle the most absurd deadlines, my thanks to Sarah Carter. To my copy editor, Helen Gray, for her insight and efficiency. To Nic, Henry, Suzanne, Clemence and the great team at Head of Zeus, for their enthusiasm and professionalism.

To my agent, John Richard Parker, for his patience, tenacity, and good humour.

My heartfelt thanks to Bill and Jill, for their encouragement, support, and grace. To my Mom and Dad, who just can't seem to give up on me.

My love and gratitude to Nana, whose stories of life

during the Blitz (like all her stories) crackled with a little mischief.

Most of all, to my wonderful wife Jackie, who inspired it all.

The Real Ravenmaster

In Conversation with Christopher Skaife,
the Tower of London's 6th Ravenmaster

How did you become Ravenmaster at the Tower of London?

To become a Yeoman Warder you have to have served a minimum of 22 years in the military, have an exemplary record, and attained the rank of warrant officer or above.

The previous Ravenmaster, Derrick Coyle, saw I was fascinated with the birds – so he put me in the cage, and it seemed they liked me, too. I was a part of his raven team for five years before taking over the job.

Did you have previous experience working with birds?

I didn't know a lot about Corvids before. I had cats, and I still do. And a dog. (Raven Alfie, he's known as the eighth raven.)

How many ravens are there?

At the moment we have seven – six by Royal Decree and one spare: Harris (Male), Merlina (Female), Munin (Female), Rocky (Male), Gripp (Male), Jubilee (Male) and the sisters Erin and Hugine. Most are quite young – Munin is our oldest, at 21 years old. The oldest raven to live at the Tower was Jim, who died at 44 years old.

Where do the Tower ravens come from?

Most of our ravens come from breeders in Somerset. Two of our birds are wild – Merlina, from South Wales, and Munin, from North Uist in Scotland.

I try to keep them as wild as possible, giving them free reign around the grounds. We've just had new open-air cages built – ravens don't belong in boxes.

What's the most difficult part of the job?

The hours. My daily routine starts at first light, where I let the ravens out, clean their cages, and prepare their food – a ration of roughly 500 grams of meat a day – mainly chicken and mouse, in addition to whatever they nick off the tourists. They are out wild during the day, though I keep an eye on them and put them to bed at nightfall.

I do all the normal duties of a Yeoman Warder, with the extra responsibility of looking after the ravens. A team of three helps me out, covering my off days when I'm not here at the Tower.

And the best part?

The ravens. It is a fabulous job to look after the ravens and learn all about them. And I get to wear the iconic uniform.

Do you have a good relationship with all of them?

I have a great relationship with all of the ravens, but they don't all have a great relationship with me. I've got scars from bites up and down my arms.

Do they get along with each other?

Merlina doesn't get on with the other ravens, which is why she has her own night-time lodgings – a special cage in the wall of the Queen's House, which makes her the princess of the Tower.

Are the ravens really as smart and 'sophisticated' as Uncle Henry says?

Ravens are extremely intelligent animals, with a complicated understanding of past, present, and future. University students come here to study their behaviour and cognitive ability, which is thought to be similar to chimps or dolphins. If humans had brains relative to the size of raven's, our heads would be twice as big. All this intelligence, of course, leads to them being very curious – and sometimes naughty, stealing purses from tourists and hiding the coins all around the grounds.

Do they ever try to escape?

They do. I mean, they can fly – I don't clip their wings (I hate that expression), I only unbalance their flight wings a little. They can still take off. Often they'll fly around the White Tower or over the Thames before coming in to go to bed. Once, I lost Merlina for 7 days. I got a call from a man in Greenwich, wondering if we'd lost a raven. I talked him through catching her – a piece of chicken, a blanket, and some gloves – and we came and got her.

Is it true that you used to live next to Bloody Tower, but had to move house because of some ghostly happenings?

That is true, though I don't strictly believe in ghosts. I do believe in what I call 'echoes of the past'. There were some strange goings on. I had a real feeling of dread. Objects missing and strange noises. It's much more peaceful where I am now.

In These Dark Wings, *the legend of the ravens – and the position of Ravenmaster – starts during the Blitz; namely, as a way for Uncle Henry to keep up Anna's hopes. Is this timeline possible?*

Almost, yes. The first Ravenmaster began just after the war, in the 50s – they were just 'Quartermasters' before that. I am the 6th Ravenmaster.

Why do you think people are so fascinated by the Tower ravens?

Lots of reasons – some people see ravens as symbolic or spiritual, or they want to paint or draw them. I use social media to put up pictures and Vines as often as I can. They really are fascinating animals, and the more time I spend with them the more fascinated I am by the ravens.

You can follow Christopher and the Tower ravens on Twitter@ravenmaster1